JESSIE LOOKED AT KNOWLTON AND NODDED.

This was their best and maybe their only chance. In one lunging movement, Knowlton was up and out of the wagon, tackling the man to the ground. Jessie followed him out. As the man fell, he dropped the big scattergun. Knowlton cracked him in the face with his fist and rendered him unconscious. Jessie picked up the gun and looked around...

LONE STAR

WESLEY ELLIS

LONE STAR

AND THE
SHOWDOWNERS

A JOVE BOOK

LONE STAR AND THE SHOWDOWNERS

A Jove Book / published by arrangement with
the author

PRINTING HISTORY
Jove edition / February 1983

ISBN: 0-515-06233-2

Jove books are published by Jove Publications, Inc.,
200 Madison Avenue, New York, N.Y. 10016. The words
"A JOVE BOOK" and the "J" with sunburst are trademarks
belonging to Jove Publications, Inc.

PRINTED IN THE UNITED STATES OF AMERICA

Chapter 1

The Nebraska countryside rolled by Jessie Starbuck's compartment window, occasionally obscured by the engine's gray, swirling smoke. Looking up from the novel she was reading, she saw the green-breasted hills pass beneath the crystalline blue of the open sky. Trees dotted the landscape, and cornfields with rows and rows of waxy green shoots rose from the dark soil. The *rattle-clack, rattle-clack* of the Pullman car along the spur line from the Union Pacific kept her on edge, though she was exhausted by the tedium of the seven-hundred-mile journey from Texas. All the while she had been fretful, distracted.

She was reading a book called *Emma* by an English lady named Jane Austen. Emma's problems—mainly concerning romance—were far removed from her own. The novel took her out of herself and turned her attention from the harsher realities of her world. She had left her beloved Circle Star ranch in Texas on a trip to an obscure Nebraska town; she wasn't certain yet what was going on in this corner of Nebraska that should concern her, but she aimed to find out presently.

With her rode her companion, Ki. The serene countenance of the half-Japanese, half-American man belied the tumultuous, often violent life he led as Jessie's right-hand man, and her best friend. His crow-black hair fell in twin locks over his forehead. His almond-shaped eyes were closed as he attempted to grab several minutes of sleep.

It had been a long journey for both of them. Jessie closed the book and laid it on her lap. The train whistle blew as they passed a small cluster of frame buildings.

The loud signal brought Ki fully awake. He looked at Jessie, whose face was furrowed in deep thought. Sensing her unease, he said, "The book does not take your spirit up as it should."

"It's not Jane Austen's fault," said Jessie, shrugging her slender shoulders. She fingered the leatherbound volume, then put it aside. "I just can't seem to relax and take my mind off the business."

"Perhaps you were not meant to take over your father's position. You're a woman in a world of men. It can't ever be easy for you."

"I realized that, Ki, from the moment I heard he was dead. But I knew then—and I know now—that there's no other place for me. After all, I'm the only living Starbuck, the only one left with his blood."

"Yes, blood." Ki sat back on the velvet-covered sofa next to her. His lean frame folded gracefully into position. "Most Americans don't place so much importance on blood ties. You're different in that way, Jessie—in many ways."

Jessie looked into the man's dark Oriental eyes. Ki had been closer to Alex Starbuck, her father, than had almost any man, as close as she had been. And she always listened

2

to his counsel, for Ki rarely spoke unless he had something important to say.

"From you, I consider that the highest compliment," she said. "You know, both of us are different, and together—well, we must seem a queer pair to most people."

He laughed softly. "I notice the stares, the sometimes hateful looks. But I'm sure they're directed at me, not at you. However little whites care for their own blood relations, they despise any mixture of that blood with foreign races. Fear and hate are never far from the surface in their thoughts. And I bring out the worst in them."

"They don't know you, Ki. Otherwise they wouldn't think like that. Besides, you're a hundred times better than most folks we run into."

Ki said nothing. Jessie was a picture at which he never tired of looking. Her hair, which in different lights changed color from deep red to shimmering gold, spilled to her shoulders; her skin was richly colored from the time she spent outdoors, but it retained its softness; and her eyes, a vivid, flashing green, conveyed the swing and depth of her emotions and her intelligence. Her classically sculptured nose and cheekbones and chin attested to her fine breeding, and the rosy curve of her lips gave her beautiful demeanor a touch of sensuality.

Usually, as now, she dressed casually—almost carelessly—in trail clothing: blue denim pants that clung tightly to thigh, calf, and buttock, emphasizing her womanly curves; low-heeled riding boots, scuffed from long use; a pale cambric blouse that hugged the contours of her breasts; and a vest which did little to hide that part of her body. Her low-crowned riding hat lay at one end of the sofa, where she had tossed it thoughtlessly.

The train chugged on, the lulling rhythm contrasting with the clacking of the wheels on the steel rails. They were silent for a while. But Ki, disturbed by Jessie's continuing morose attitude, broke that silence. "Your father would not

3

be pleased to see you behave so. What is bothering you?"

Jessie sighed. "If I knew, I'd tell you, Ki. It's just a feeling I have. Something is going on in Gilead, but I don't know what. And I don't like not knowing. Especially where company business is concerned."

For over a year now, Ki had seen the young woman become absorbed by the Starbuck family enterprises, the legacy of her brilliant father, who had been brutally assassinated by his enemies. It was a formidable and dangerous task for anyone to tackle, let alone a young woman. But Jessie was determine to follow in Alex Starbuck's footsteps, to fulfill his life's work by carrying on his business interests. It was never an easy job, and was often an immensely heavy burden for her to bear, but she had nonetheless proved her strength and courage time and again. It was clear to Ki that she had inherited much of her father's fortitude, cleverness, and business acumen. And slowly but surely, others were seeing it too—including the foreign cartel which had hoped to break the Starbuck company after the death of its founder.

Jessie never let up, though. And she had not forgotten that it was that very cartel, an alliance of unscrupulous business competitors, which was responsible for Alex Starbuck's death. It was the opportunity to wreak vengeance on the killers, as much as anything else, that kept her going.

Nor could Ki himself forget the great man for whom he would have gladly given his own life if it had been possible to save him. Cut down in a rain of lead, ambushed on a deserted road by an army of cowards, Alex Starbuck had been snuffed out coldly and efficiently, without a chance to fight back. That was typical of the methods of his enemies. Like jungle animals, they were vicious, predatory, instinctively murderous in their methods. Along with Jessie, Ki would never rest until he saw them decisively defeated, their evil agents smashed, their business interests disrupted and ruined....

4

"We shall find out in Gilead, Jessie. But until we get there, there's no point in your brooding over it."

"Of course, Ki," she said, smiling warmly for the first time in days. "With my father gone, you're the only one I can count on to talk sense to me. Have I told you recently how much I appreciate you?"

"Not since last week," Ki joked. "But I'm like a cat, I don't need to be petted all the time. I'm what you call self-contained."

The young woman laughed out loud. "Oh, Ki—how right you are. I've never known a man as independent as you are. Perhaps our friend Longarm can match you—but no one else."

"Your Marshal Long is indeed a unique man. He's unlike most Americans. He lives by a code of honor, and he respects the lives of others. That is rare, even for so-called lawmen."

"Unfortunately, that is true. I wish Longarm were here in Nebraska. Maybe he'd have some idea what this mystery is all about. I'm anxious to talk to this Mr. Kelso, first off. He didn't answer my reply to his wire. I hope nothing is wrong, but I have a feeling..."

Ki, who relied as much upon gut feeling and an acquired inner logic as upon physical strength and prowess, understood what Jessie meant. His training in the Japans, where he grew up and was taught the way of the *bushi* by a veteran samurai, had emphasized equally the inner resources and the physical conditioning of the true warrior. And he had not survived as long as he had in this strange country without adhering to the tenets of that training.

"We will know soon enough," he said simply.

At Gilead they disembarked from their Pullman car at a small, lonely station on the east side of town. Jessie and Ki hired a man to take their luggage to the Whittington Hotel, across Center Street from the county courthouse.

They then went straight to the Starbuck Enterprises office. The evening was cool and pleasant, and as they walked they enjoyed the freedom of being on their feet once again and out of the confines of the railroad car.

The office was on the first floor of a two-story frame building with a high false front. Jessie peered inside the front window, and by the light of a kerosene lamp she could see someone inside—a portly older woman sweeping the floor. Jessie's knock brought the woman to the door.

"Hullo, may I help you?" the woman said, easing open the door just far enough to stick her head out.

"I'm Jessica Starbuck, ma'am. I've come to see Mr. Kelso." She could see a look of distrust in the woman's eyes. "Is he in?"

"Starbuck? You a real Starbuck?"

"I'm my father's daughter. And he was Alex Starbuck."

"*The* Mr. Starbuck?" The woman pushed a stray strand of silver hair off her forehead. "Well, I never. Then you own this place. Not much I can do to keep you out of here if you own the place. Not much at all. Come in, come in. I'm just cleaning up." She opened the door to admit Jessie and Ki, staring suspiciously at the half-Japanese man.

"Is *he* with you, Miss Starbuck?" she queried.

"Of course. This is Ki. And you are—"

"I'm Mrs. Oxbridge. I was Mr. Kelso's landlady. I decided to clean up his office here. I didn't realize he was so disorganized. Papers and trash all over the place—what a mess! Ah, but it was a pleasure to know him, poor man."

"What happened to him?" Jessie didn't like the woman's tone; she was talking as if the man were no longer around.

"Oh, dear. You asked for Mr. Kelso. I'm sorry. I guess I should have told you. I'm not used to it myself. He's dead."

"Dead?" Jessie's heart leaped into her throat. Her worst fear had been realized. "When did he die? How did it happen, Mrs. Oxbridge?"

6

"Poor man. Just when he was finding happiness in his work, something to live for. His wife died five years ago, you know. Left him broken, uninterested in anything. But the past several weeks—it was as if he had suddenly got back his will to live. And then this."

"Please, Mrs. Oxbridge," Jessie insisted. "Tell me what happened."

"I'm surprised you didn't know about it. I sent a wire to—or did I? My, there have been so many things to do recently. Perhaps I didn't get to the telegraph office after all. I'm sorry."

Mrs. Oxbridge was a stout woman in her late fifties. She wore a wide apron around her generous midsection and had her sleeves rolled up to reveal fleshy but strong arms. Her face was weathered and wrinkled, her eyes a pale brown and filled with concern. An ample bosom gave her the appearance of maternal warmth and seemed to be the cause of her slight stoop. She rested on the broomstick, looking from Jessie to Ki. "I've been so busy here, cleaning up the place. I was sure—"

"Start from the beginning, please," Jessie told her. "Would you care to sit down?"

"Yes, I think I will." Ki brought her a chair and the landlady sat down with a heavy sigh. "Thank you kindly." She nodded at Ki, still uncertain what to make of his disconcerting Oriental features and manner.

Jessie cleared space on a nearby desktop and sat down herself as Ki drifted toward the front door to keep watch on the street. A cloud of mystery and danger had descended upon the room. "Now," the young woman encouraged Mrs. Oxbridge, "just tell me everything you know about when and how Mr. Kelso died. Please don't leave out anything. It's very important."

"All right." Mrs. Oxbridge took a handkerchief from her bosom and wiped her face. "It was last week. Like I said, the poor man was just getting back on his feet after all the

7

bad times. Now he never neglected his business, Miss Star-buck—he was a fine and loyal worker and I'm sure you'll find the records here all in order—but his heart wasn't in it since his wife passed. It was the influenza. He nursed her through it all, poor man. I did all I could, but he insisted on being at her side most of the time. They didn't have any children. I suppose that was a blessing, as it turned out. He came to live at my boardinghouse shortly after she died."

Jessie, impatient as she was, decided not to hurry the woman, to let her tell the story in her own way.

Mrs. Oxbridge captured another wild strand of hair and pinned it behind her ear. "Well, like I said, it happened last week. For some reason, Mr. Kelso was all excited, more interested in his work than at any time since the poor girl's death. He kept telling me that he had made a great discov-ery—though he never said what it was exactly. He was always here late, reading books and writing things down. And he was out very often during the day. He said he went over to Beacon—that's a little town twenty miles or so from here. I couldn't make out what it was all about, but he seemed happier than I'd seen him in a long while."

Jessie glanced over her shoulder at Ki, who stood cas-ually at the front door. He acknowledged her with a nod, then turned his attention to the street outside; he had the feeling that someone had been watching them ever since they stepped off the train. And it never paid to ignore such quiet signals of danger.

"He telegraphed about that discovery," Jessie told Mrs. Oxbridge. "That's why I'm here. I wanted to find out from Mr. Kelso himself exactly what it was."

"Oh, my, I'm afraid you've come a long way for nothing, then. I haven't the faintest idea. Only Mr. Kelso knew. And he didn't tell a soul, I don't think." The older woman smoothed her apron with work-roughened red hands. "I'm terribly sorry."

8

"But please tell us about his death, Mrs. Oxbridge," Jessie prodded her.

"Yes, well, it's very unpleasant. I discovered his body. The next morning. You see, he often worked late, especially with this new project. Sometimes I brought him over breakfast, and I'd find him asleep in his office. That's what I thought had happened at first when I came in. It was last Monday. He was at his desk, slumped over. I thought I'd let him sleep some as I tidied up, but I noticed that he wasn't snoring. And he was a terrible one for snoring. My late husband was too, you know. Anyhow, when I finally decided to wake him for a cup of coffee—that's when I saw the blood. He'd been shot in the lower back three times."

She dabbed her rheumy eyes with a handkerchief. "Poor man. The office had been looted. I don't know how much money he'd kept there, but there was none left. I called the county sheriff over—there's no town marshal in Gilead—and he said it was a clear case of robbery and murder. But he hasn't found out who did it. I haven't heard from him since that day. I don't know who could have done such an awful thing. Mr. Kelso never harmed a soul. He was such a nice, quiet man."

"I'd like to take a look around his office, if you don't mind," said Jessie.

"Lord, no. It's yours, after all. Follow me." Mrs. Oxbridge led her back, stopping to light another lamp. She unlocked the door and stepped inside the dim, dingy room.

Kelso had apparently resisted Mrs. Oxbridge's attempts to tidy his domain. There were books and papers and charts stacked everywhere, as well as boxes and tools and rolled-up maps scattered over the floor and on chairs. The office itself was small, fifteen-by-fifteen, with frosted glass windows behind the cluttered desk. She went to the chair, which was still bloodstained.

"The sheriff told me not to touch anything, Miss Star-

9

buck, until he had finished his investigation. So I haven't."
The woman looked rather sheepish, as if she wanted to clear
out the entire mess and scrub down the walls and make the
place shine.

"That's all right," Jessie said, her eyes scanning every
inch of the place, looking for clues. She inspected the ma-
terial on the desk. She found the scribbled draft of the wire
she had received from Kelso: *Important find in Beacon,
Neb. Merits Starbuck attention. Will discuss with appropriate company representative. Yours truly, Dudley Kelso.*
Cryptic and fascinating, the telegraph message meant a hell
of a lot more, she knew, than it said.

Taking the lamp from Mrs. Oxbridge, Jessie placed it
on the desk and sat in the dead man's chair. She was trying
to recreate what he was doing at the time of his murder.
Right in front of her was a book, *The Discovery of Petroleum
in North America, Being a Natural History and Survey
Compiled by the Geological Society of the United States.*

The older woman saw the book and said, "That was Mr.
Kelso's bible. He carried it around with him everywhere he
went. He must have read it through a dozen times."

"It looks like he was reading it when they killed him,"
Jessie said tonelessly, wondering how Kelso's discovery—
whatever it was—tied in with his sudden death. Flipping
through the pages of the book, she saw that he had under-
scored several passages.

Ki, meanwhile, continued his watch at the front of the
Starbuck company office. Ever alert to the slightest sound
or movement, he was convinced that someone was approaching—but he could not see who it was, or from where
the person was coming. So he went to extinguish the lantern
and cast the outer office into darkness, the better to see into
the deepening gloom of the street. He stationed himself
beside the door once again, his eyes sweeping up and down
the street. He saw nothing—yet the premonition of danger

10

remained with him, as palpable to him as a noxious odor or dull ache in the head.

Ki had the height of his American forebears, and was wiry of build, with long, straight black hair that framed his Oriental features. He wore tight-fitting denim pants, a collarless cotton shirt that allowed him freedom of movement, a battered leather vest with many pockets, and a pair of rope-soled cotton slippers. Even in this rough country, he had no need of boots, his feet having been toughened by his lifelong training as a warrior. In fact, he found heavy footwear a hindrance; he liked to be able to feel every nuance of the ground under his feet.

Even after living in this country for several years, Ki still did not understand Americans' values. Money and raw power were all that seemed to matter—and how they were acquired was unimportant. Human life was cheap, especially out West, where men were killed every day without reason or purpose, but simply because they stood in the way of others. Sometimes Ki could not keep down the disgust that built in him like a fever. But, governed by the *bushido* code of conduct, he fought to control those impulses within himself. It was not easy, but he had made it his life's purpose to live and die honorably in the service of his master, Alex Starbuck, who lived on in his beautiful daughter, Jessica. He knew no more honorable people than the Starbucks, and he was proud to serve them.

The half-Japanese warrior carried no firearms; he found guns heavy and cumbersome and noisy—the white man's folly. Although he admired skill with any weapon, he preferred the traditional arms of his country: the long-bladed *katana* sword, the samurai's best friend; the shorter *wakazashi* blade; the long bow and its *ebira* quiver, filled with deadly war arrows; the *nunchaku,* consisting of two hardwood sticks joined by a length of horsehair; and the silent, dangerous throwing stars called *shuriken*. There were dozens of other strange weapons he could use—strange, that is, to Westerners, who did not appreciate subtlety or beauty in a fighting man's weapons. The round-eyes preferred force over beauty, brute action over skilled movement.

Now he carried only his *ko-dachi* in a belt sheath, and several *shuriken* stars in his vest pockets.

A scream—it sounded like Mrs. Oxbridge's voice raised in terror—erupted from Kelso's office. Ki turned and bounded to the door, knowing that his fears had been realized. He pushed open the door and saw two men, armed and bandanna-masked, who had broken in through the back window. One held a revolver to Jessie's head, the other a shotgun on Mrs. Oxbridge, who was quivering and about to collapse from fright.

Ki caught Jessie's eye. She nodded almost imperceptibly; she knew what to do. The man behind her jabbed the gun into the back of her neck and she winced. Ki cursed inwardly. The man was as good as dead. Already Ki palmed a shiny disk, a *shuriken* throwing star. He stood stock-still, awaiting his chance to use it.

"Don't try anything funny, Chinaman," said the other man. He prodded Mrs. Oxbridge with the black barrel of the big shotgun. She stumbled a few steps forward. She beseeched Ki with her eyes to obey the intruder.

"Darrel," said the man behind Jessie—a tall, skinny, gravel-voiced hardcase—"set the old lady down and check this fellow out. Grandma ain't goin' nowhere."

The second man, the one called Darrel, burly and slow-moving, obeyed the other's command. He eased the older woman down to the floor with the gunbarrel. Mrs. Oxbridge kneeled, cowering under the weight of the weapon. Darrel stepped around her, keeping the gun leveled at Ki's gut.

Ki glanced again at Jessie—now was the time. The blade fell to his slender fingertips. Then, suddenly, Jessie fell to the floor, leaving the hardcase exposed. In confusion, the masked man looked down; and Darrel was distracted for a split second, turning to see what was happening. In a swift, graceful movement that was quicker that the eye could take in, Ki launched the *shuriken* star at the man. The throwing blade flashed across the room, and the sharp edges cut into the intruder's neck, slicing through his Adam's apple. A gurgled cry came from his mouth as blood spurted from the severed windpipe, spilling in a crimson cascade down the front of his shirt. His masked head twisted violently and he dropped his revolver.

Jessie spun and recovered the weapon, rolling away as the man tumbled onto the wooden floor beside her.

As soon as Ki released the star, he turned and stepped outside the door. The second intruder, Darrel, recovered and cut loose with his scattergun.

The explosion was deafening, and lead sprayed through the open door and pitted the wall opposite. But Ki had ducked away from the door. In the next room he saw the broom that Mrs. Oxbridge had used to sweep the floor. He lunged for it just as the man came through the door. Darrel had to jump aside as Jessie, from behind the desk, thumbed back the hammer on the revolver and sent a bullet crashing after him. Ki felt the broom handle in his grasp as he leaped forward into the room, away from the black barrel of Darrel's shotgun. The hardcase took aim and fired. Blue-orange flame spat forth and hot lead exploded at Ki as he crabbed to the left.

He took some grains of shot in his right arm, but luckily that was all. The pain bit him, but he ignored it. He stood, knowing that the man had used both barrels and must reload. The hardcase knew it too, and cracked open the chambers, fumbling in his pocket for shells. Ki gave him no time to put another shell into the gun. He jumped toward the man, wielding the broomstick like a short *bo,* one of his favorite weapons. Confronting the startled intruder, Ki executed a savage overhead stroke that knocked the scattergun from Darrel's hands.

13

Darrel went for his handgun, a short-barreled .45 Colt, yanking it from a low-slung holster on his left side. He was quicker than Ki had anticipated. He got off a single shot that whistled past Ki's shoulder. Ki advanced, holding the stick in the ready position, his left hand across the chest, palm outward, grasping the broom and his right hand at his side, wrapped tightly around the stick. He kicked and whirled, avoiding a second bullet that whanged into the ceiling above his head. Then he brought the broomstick in a vicious uppercut, slashing under the masked gunman's wrist. With a howl, Darrel released the revolver, which spun into the air and fell clattering to the floor.

Ki snapped the stick around at gut level, punching the hardcase in the kidney. Darrel grunted and grabbed madly for the stick, almost knocking it away. His eyes shone with anger and vengeance above the bandanna that covered the lower part of his face. He wasn't about to give up. He stepped to his left, narrowly avoiding another sideways blow from Ki. Then he came over the top of the stick with his fist leading. Ki recovered his balance and swung the broomstick up under the man's armpit. Darrel yelped and withdrew. Ki then feinted a blow to Darrel's midsection, doubling the man over, and followed with a strong smash to the side of his face.

Jessie had come out of the office, revolver in hand, to help Ki. She saw, though, that her companion was in control of the situation.

His cheekbone cracked, blood trickling from his ear, Darrel reeled drunkenly. Ki stepped forward and planted the end of the broom handle under the hardcase's chin. He thrust it hard, snapping Darrel's head back and pushing him backward over a chair. The intruder went sprawling, his head crashing on the floor, rendering him unconscious.

Jessie sprang forward. "Ki! Are you all right?" As he stood there regaining his breath, she saw the bloodied arm where buckshot had torn through his skin. She touched it gingerly and he winced. "It doesn't look too bad. I'll clean it up for you."

From inside Kelso's office the two of them heard Mrs. Oxbridge sobbing. Jessie went to tend to her as Ki bent over the man called Darrel. He ripped away the mask. The man was young, in his mid-twenties, his face pitted and scarred, probably from a childhood bout with smallpox. He searched his pockets for papers, but only came up with about twenty dollars and a handful of shotgun shells.

After Jessie had calmed the frightened woman, Ki searched the dead man. He plucked his *shuriken* blade from the man's neck and wiped it clean on the hardcase's shirt before replacing it in his own vest. Like Darrel, this one carried no form of identification. And his face, after the mask was removed, was unfamiliar. Mrs. Oxbridge, when she could speak coherently again, said she had not seen the two men before.

Jessie said, "I have a feeling, though, that they've been here before—the night Mr. Kelso was killed."

"You think—" Mrs. Oxbridge breathed. "You think *they* murdered him?"

"The one in the front room will be able to talk after a few hours. Perhaps he can be persuaded to answer some questions," Ki said.

"Let's haul him over to the sheriff's office," Jessie suggested. "He'll probably find a jail cell more comfortable than this cold floor."

"Oh, my," Mrs. Oxbridge moaned, wiping her hands on her apron. "I'm afraid you two haven't been made properly welcome here in Gilead. I'm so sorry."

"It's not your fault, ma'am." Jessie placed a comforting hand on the older woman's shoulder. "Why don't you go on home now."

"I suppose I should see to dinner over at the boardinghouse. I'll have some hungry boarders by now. But this place is more of a mess than when I started. Have you seen my broom? I thought I left it over there by the door."

Jessie and Ki laughed. "You'll have plenty of time to clean up tomorrow," Jessie said. "And I'm sure your broom will turn up."

★

Chapter 2

Jessie asked Mrs. Oxbridge to alert the local undertaker to the fact that he had a body to take care of. Then they picked up the limp form of the hardcase named Darrel and trundled him out into the street. He was heavy, and Jessie worried that Ki's flesh wound would start bleeding again.

From a passing stranger, Jessie asked for the location of the sheriff's office and was told it was down the street from the county courthouse, three blocks away. She and Ki passed that impressive limestone structure, the roof of which was supported by massive pillars. There was even a new bronze statue of Justice on the front lawn. As the county seat of Box Butte County, Gilead held an important position among the other, smaller towns in the area. It was always a coveted stamp of distinction to be designated the county seat, and Gilead wore that distinction with pride.

As befitted his position, the sheriff was headquartered in

a clean, whitewashed brick building, part of which served as jailhouse. A group of idlers milled about on the boardwalk outside the door, which was painted green and clearly marked, OFFICE OF THE SHERIFF, BOX BUTTE COUNTY. The men parted to allow Jessie and Ki to pass, lifting their hats to the lady and eyeing her companion; they did not hide their hostile curiosity about his Oriental features and strange garb.

Their limp bundle began to stir. He opened his eyes just as they entered the place, blinking them rapidly. His arms and legs took on life and he began to struggle with his captors. "What the hell is this? Where am I?"

Jessie and Ki dropped him to the floor with a thud. As he lay there, he began to recollect the battle in Kelso's office. "Where's my pal Jimbo? What did you do to Jimbo?"

"Jimbo's dead, friend," Jessie said evenly.

Just then a skinny, stooped man with thinning gray hair came up to them, scratching his head. Dry white flakes flew at the touch of his soiled fingers. He wore a sweat-stained shirt and corduroy pants. An ill-used revolver hung at his side in a cracked leather holster, and a tarnished star was pinned to the front of his shirt. "Now, what's all this brou-haha?"

He looked down at the writhing Darrel, then to Jessie and Ki. His rheumy eyes and nervous hands, as well as his reeking breath, betrayed a love of alcohol. He looked the type who'd rather drink than eat, rather drink than ride, rather drink than make money. Jessie had seen lawmen like him, and she didn't like what she saw. It sickened her. She introduced herself and Ki.

"Why, a—a pleasure, ma'am." He reached up as if to lift his hat, discovered that he wasn't wearing it, and dropped his hand to his pocket. "I'm the sheriff hereabouts, ma'am. Bob Lowell is my name. Pleasured to make your acquaintance."

"Do you know this man?" Jessie asked him, pointing to the downed hardcase.

Lowell peered intently at Darrel, summoning his frayed power of concentration, squinting his watery eyes. "Cain't say as I do. What has he gone and done?"

Jessie explained how Darrel and the man called Jimbo broke into the Starbuck office and threatened their lives. She told him that they had killed the second man, and the sheriff winced. It was clear that he didn't like trouble and wasn't equipped to handle such situations. But Jessie pressed on. "We want you to lock this one up after we've had a chance to question him some. Think you can do that, Sheriff Lowell?"

"Well...I s'pose I oughta, if'n you say so, ma'am. Cain't have him runnin' loose, causin' trouble for folks."

Exasperated by this timid, puppy-dog attitude, Jessie said, "Look, Sheriff, if you don't handle this, we will. This man more than likely had something to do with Mr. Kelso's death. Doesn't that interest you?"

Lowell fidgeted and grimaced; sweat poured down his creased, pale forehead. "Now I've done all I could about Mr. Kelso. Ain't found nothin' solid as yet. But I'm workin' on it, ma'am. 'Pears to me that these fellas wouldn'a stuck around if'n they killed Mr. Kelso. But you want this man throwed in jail, I'll throw him for ya. Makes no never-mind to me."

"I want more than that," Jessie fumed. "I want to know just what you've done to find out who killed Kelso—and why."

Taking advantage of their distracted attention, Darrel bolted for the door. In one quick step, Ki was behind him, grabbing the outlaw's shirt collar and yanking him to his knees. One powerful, side-handed chop to Darrel's neck silenced him and rendered him an unconscious heap.

Sheriff Lowell watched this with an open mouth, glancing from Ki to Jessie and back to Ki again. "Why, I never seed nothin' like that," he mumbled. "Best git him into a cell for his own pertection."

Jessie cursed silently. This addle-brained, bottle-sucking lawman was going to be of absolutely no help. How could such an incompetent be elected in the first place, she wondered, unless there were payoffs and political manuevering somewhere along the way. She supposed that was how it happened here, because that was how it happened elsewhere. And now she and Ki were stuck dealing with this drunken star-toter. In other words, they'd have to conduct their own investigation and hope for no interference—and no help—from Lowell.

"He's in no shape for us to question him tonight, Ki," Jessie said. "We better leave him here. We'll be back tomorrow, Sheriff," she added.

"Why, of course . . . no harm . . . I mean, sure, I'll do what I can. See, I ain't got no deputies, so I have to do it all myself. Just don't have time to cover the whole county. Wisht I could hire me another man or two." His face sagged as he told his sad story, hoping for some sympathy from the two strangers. He didn't get any.

"What's stopping you from hiring a deputy?" asked Jessie.

"Well, Mr. Winslow—that is, the people in the county haven't seed fit to give me enough money to hire on another man. Not much I can do about it," the hapless sheriff whined.

Jessie and Ki didn't miss his slip of the tongue. *Winslow*. They'd discover soon enough who he was—and how he controlled Lowell's pursestrings. For now, they'd leave the sheriff to his bottle and his private nightmares.

They set out for Mrs. Oxbridge's boardinghouse, to see how she was holding up after the incident. Her establishment was a freshly painted two-story house near the middle of town, set off from the street by a picket fence. Bright curtains hung in the windows, and flowers and hedges adorned the front lawn. All in all, it looked like a prosperous setup. They went to the front door and knocked.

A young woman opened the door. Her rich black hair fell to her shoulders. The light from inside the house silhouetted her figure; she wore a loose shirt and tight-fitting pants and riding boots. Behind her, Jessie and Ki heard the sounds of people dining.

Mrs. Oxbridge called out: "Tell them to come in, Yvonne! I'll be right out."

The girl said hello and invited them in. She spoke with a quiet voice but did not regard them shyly. Especially Ki. She looked him over with frank interest. What an odd-looking and handsome man! Immediately she wondered where he was from and what he was like. And she wondered if he was this other woman's man. Her heart dropped at the thought, for she had never seen anyone like Ki in Gilead. Here all the men were old and worn out and bent over, or else they were uncouth cattlemen or drummers or, worst of all, preachers. She was taken aback at the sight of a man like Ki, and she determined to get to know him better—as soon as possible.

Mrs. Oxbridge came out and greeted Jessie and Ki with a motherly embrace. "Did you take that awful man to jail? Are you hungry? You must be tired. Come, I'm serving supper now. Yvonne, set two more places at the table." The girl went to do as she was told, and Mrs. Oxbridge guided her two guests into the dining room before they had a chance to protest.

Jessie looked at Ki and smiled. They were, indeed, as hungry as a pair of horses. Though they were anxious to get back to their hotel and crawl into bed, they could not refuse the lady's offer of a meal. And Ki, for his part, was intrigued by the girl, Yvonne, and sensed that she was equally curious about him. If he knew anything about women, he knew the signals they sent out when they were attracted to a man. Even one as young as this girl—and he guessed

21

she was about seventeen—was capable of emitting those signals, almost by instinct.

The table was laden abundantly with food: a big pink ham, corn on the cob, boiled potatoes, bright green snap beans, biscuits, butter, honey, gravy, a pitcher of milk, pots of coffee. Two men sat opposite each other, busily shoveling food from their plates to their mouths. They looked up long enough to greet Jessie and Ki, then returned to their meal.

One man, a young-looking fellow with bright red hair and freckles, was Donald Rumston, a drummer; the other, a rather stout, dour-faced man of about fifty, with a double chin, was introduced as Peter Staniels, a local attorney.

Jessie and Ki sat down as Yvonne brought plates and silverware. Mrs. Oxbridge bustled about, making sure they were comfortable and dishing out large servings of food. She stood back, wiping her hands on her ever-present apron, to watch them eat. Hungry after their long day, the two guests responded heartily, making short work of their supper.

Rumston, washing down the last of his potatoes with a tall glass of fresh milk, said, "I declare, Mrs. Oxbridge sets the best table this side of Omaha. I tell all my customers that if they're ever in Gilead, this is the place to stay. Cheaper and cleaner than any hotel, that's for sure." He grinned, his freckles dancing on his face.

"Thank you, Mr. Rumston," the landlady said.

Staniels, the lawyer, grunted in assent, wiping his plate with a buttered biscuit. He looked up inquiringly at Mrs. Oxbridge.

The older lady turned to Yvonne, who hovered near Ki, unable to detach her gaze from his intriguing features. "I believe we're ready for the rhubarb pie. Be a dear and fetch it in, Yvonne. Mr. Staniels is about to faint from lack of pie. Coffee, Mr. Staniels?" She poured him a full cup of the steaming brew.

Jessie had to smile. Already she felt a deep affection for

the kindly boardinghouse keeper, and she appreciated Mrs. Oxbridge's ability to carry on after the frightening confrontation in the Starbuck company office. Biting into a delicious, warm biscuit, she was surprised when the red-haired drummer spoke to her.

"Pardon my asking, ma'am," he said, "but are you in Gilead for business or pleasure? The reason I say that is, maybe, if it's business, I could be of some assistance. You see, in my line I get to know pretty much everybody in a town like Gilead. Just thought I'd tell you." He blushed deeply. He was smitten with the beautiful but roughly dressed young woman. Valiantly, he maintained a cool smile.

"Thank you, Mr. Rumston," Jessie said. "I'll keep your offer in mind. Ki and I are here on family business."

Yvonne carried in golden deep-dish pie and set it down on the table. Mrs. Oxbridge carved generous slices with a gleaming knife. Attorney Staniels attacked his piece with relish, seemingly ignoring the others' talk. But Jessie could tell that, despite his apparent inattention, he was hearing everything that was said.

"I'm in notions and sundries," Rumston went on, trying to keep Jessie's ear.

"Is business good?" she asked.

"Oh, couldn't be better," he responded, beaming. "If I do say so myself, I think I'm a pretty good salesman. Here's my card." He flumbled in his coat pocket for a moment and produced an engraved business card, reaching across the table to hand it to her.

Meanwhile, Ki quietly finished his meal. He drank a cup of strong coffee, half wishing that he had a hot cup of green tea instead. At times like this, his thoughts wandered far, remembering the sights and sounds and smells of the Japans, the island country he had left so long ago. To him, America was still a foreign, uncultured place. He often longed for a chance to return—if only for a brief visit—to the faraway land where he had grown up, where he had trained as a warrior, where he had cultivated the finer aspects of life. In this country, he had found, there was no appreciation for beauty and order, for art and precision. Only in the person of Jessie's father, Alex Starbuck, had he sensed a spirit attuned to the ways of the East. That, in part, was what had set Starbuck apart from other men: the quiet, deep-flowing conviction that there was more to life than getting by or just making money or just killing to get what you want. Ki missed that; he missed Alex Starbuck. Jessie was his only link to the past that he cherished so much. To her he was bound by a special brand of love and respect—and he always would be.

Returning to the present, he sensed the girl, Yvonne, staring at him. Ki looked across the table, his eyes meeting hers. She looked away, her pretty face coloring at his direct gaze. Something stirred inside him. He realized that he hadn't had a woman in weeks. And he found himself wondering if the same thing was on her mind.

Staniels excused himself after two helpings of the pie. Jessie continued to exchange small talk with Rumston. Ki heard Yvonne talking to Mrs. Oxbridge.

"There's a carnival show in town," the girl said excitedly. "A lot of people over there at the lot next to the courthouse. They set up tents and everything earlier today." In her eyes, Yvonne displayed the innocent eagerness and curiosity of a child—and Mrs. Oxbridge saw it.

"I can't have you strolling around over there by yourself. A young lady doesn't do such things." The older woman looked to Jessie. "Does she, Miss Starbuck?"

Jessie laughed, seeing in the girl a lot of herself at the same age—which wasn't that many years ago. "I suppose not, Mrs. Oxbridge, but there can't be a shortage of boys to escort Yvonne."

"That's the only trouble," Yvonne put in. "There are plenty of *boys,* most of them dumb and dirty and smelling like cowshit."

"Yvonne!" Mrs. Oxbridge exclaimed. "Where did you learn such language?"

"From those very same 'boys,'" said the girl with an angelic smile.

Then Ki spoke up. "I'll look out for her," he said. He had been watching Yvonne with increasing interest. She was young, but she displayed the beauty and wit of a blossoming woman. And Ki hadn't enjoyed a woman's company—except Jessie's—for a while. Besides, what better way to explore the town and see the faces of the people who might know something about Kelso's murder?

"That's nice of you, Mr. Ki. But you must be tired, after your journey and all the excitement."

Ki was weary, but his mind was made up—as was Yvonne's.

"No buts about it, Mrs. Oxbridge," she said. "Mr. Ki and I are going to the carnival. I'll go upstairs and change. Be down in a minute." She bolted from the dining room.

Her hands on her wide hips, the older woman shook her head. "These girls today. They're always rushing around to dances and parties. Why, when I was young, my mother never let me out of the house—too much work to do."

"Doesn't Yvonne have any parents?" Jessie asked.

"My cousin Opal was her mother," Mrs. Oxbridge said, an edge of sadness in her voice. "She and her husband, Yvonne's father, were killed three years ago in a train robbery. Just senseless. Poor girl—I'm the only family she has now, and Lord knows I'm not always up to it."

"Looks like you've done a good job so far," Jessie reassured her. "She's a good girl."

The drummer, Rumston, excused himself at this point, reminding Jessie that he was at her service anytime she needed him. And just as he left, Yvonne came downstairs.

She wore a long-sleeved white blouse and a riding skirt, and boots that made her appear a few inches taller. Her black hair was pulled back in a tight bun at her neck. The large, dark eyes seemed larger and darker in contrast to her alabaster skin. And the way she was dressed added a few years to her age, giving her a maturity and an allure that she hadn't displayed just moments earlier. She and Ki left Jessie and Mrs. Oxbridge at the table and went out.

Yvonne was dying to know everything about Ki—where he came from, why he was with Jessie, what he was doing in Gilead. He answered her questions briefly but politely.

"What was it like for you, growing up?" she asked as they walked across the darkened street.

How could he explain to her what it had been like? His American father's tragic death, followed quickly by his Japanese mother's own end—leaving the young "mongrel" boy to find his way in a hostile world. He remembered the scorn on other boys' faces, the feel of shopkeepers' sandals on his backside, the taste of cold discarded rice. Then his fortunes had changed, though he was slow in realizing it. One night he encountered a poor, discredited samurai who, instead of killing him for the sport of it, took the boy in. The big, fierce-visaged man was called Hirata, and he became Ki's mentor and protector through the many years it took to master the way of the warrior. From the gruff and exacting Hirata the boy learned *kyujutsu, kenjutsu, bojutsu, jojutsu,* and *shuriken-jutsu*—the arts of the bow, the sword, the staff, the fighting stick, and the throwing dagger— among other martial skills. He also learned an attitude, a way of looking at the world, that was unique to this class of Nipponese warrior, the samurai. Ten years they spent together . . . ten years that had shaped Ki's life.

"Hirata was a powerful samurai and a wise man," he told Yvonne. "He knew both victory and defeat in the service of his lord. He was poor when I met him, but I later realized that he was rich in the only measure of wealth that counts— the respect of his fellow man and his comrades in arms. I learned much from him. And I mourn him to this day."

"That's sad," the girl said.

"Yes, but from sadness we often reap much happiness. I am happy that he lived and that he was my master. That is the way he taught me."

Yvonne looked up at her companion. The handsome lines of his face—the lines, both subtle and strong, that defined his power and appeal—and the dark, almond-shaped eyes and the tense leanness of his body made her go weak in the core of her womanhood. She wondered what it would be like to make love to this man.

"You must think this town and all of us in it are pretty dull," she said. "I guess you wouldn't be here if it wasn't important to you and Miss Starbuck."

"What matters is that we *are* here," said Ki.

They reached the carnival grounds and found themselves among a lively crowd of men and women from the town, eager to taste the excitement that this traveling show had to offer them.

Ki and Yvonne stood in a knot of people in front of a medicine wagon and listened to Dr. Elihu Keith's pitch for his Indian Root Miracle Tonic and Household Cleaner.

". . . Cures what ails you and protects from mosquitoes, plagues, fevers, and humors of malevolence so common here among white Americans. Concocted with strict adherence to principles of medicine ancient and modern, my unique tonic has met with astounding success both in the States and abroad, where, at the request of kings, queens, and princes, I have made it available to folks just like you. And let me tell you, those foreigners have a lot more problems than you or I, ladies and gentlemen. Yet, I've heard tell, my Indian root cure has been known to have positive effects on corruptions both of the soul and the mind. Of course, I could acquire a fortune in Europe and Asia if I so chose; but, dear people, my loyalties lie first with my own countrymen. And it would be amiss, perhaps traitorous, if I did not remain among you to preach the gospel of good health and cleanliness and offer to you this miraculous elixir

27

at an incredibly low price of just six bits per twelve-ounce bottle.

"Now I'm sure you'll want a bottle, so I must ask you to make an orderly queue right over here. And please, have your money ready. Also, I am available for brief private consultations at all hours of the day and night for the easily affordable fee of ten cents. Now, ladies and gentlemen, please step forward for Dr. Keith's Indian Root Miracle Tonic—don't push, my good woman, there's enough for everyone. Limit three bottles per customer. God bless you, sir, you won't regret it. Thank you for the correct change. Next! Step up quickly."

Yvonne had to hide her smile with her hand. "Do you believe a word he says, Ki?"

"No. I doubt whether he does himself."

They watched as the "doctor" sold a dozen bottles of his cure before they moved on. Ki could not figure out why Americans let themselves be so easily talked into spending their hard-earned money on worthless products. He supposed that flattery of the sort that Keith employed was too much for them to resist. Still, you'd think they would be reluctant to part with six bits on the strength of such a dubious presentation.

Next they came to a place where a sizable crowd was gathered around what Ki recognized as a boxing ring. This was a rarity in a time when public displays of pugilism were often outlawed, and organized fisticuffs were usually confined to private clubs. The characteristic canvas-floored square was set up on a low platform, and was now populated by a cluster of men. One of them, a man of average height with broad shoulders and long, muscular arms, was bare from the waist up, and wore only a pair of tight blue pants and high-topped, laced boots. The other men smoked cigars and shouted at each other; finally they broke up and made their way out of the ring, leaving only a short, plump, balding man in a pinstriped coat who held up his hands and called out for everyone's kind attention. Like the snake-oil dealer, he got it.

"Ladies and gentlemen, tonight you are going to witness the finest pugilistic talent you have ever seen in a challenge match in the heavyweight class. Dennis Heany, undefeated in forty professional fights, has consented to a series of exhibition bouts throughout the West in which he shall take on all comers in his weight class. The American Carnival Entertainment Company offers twenty-five dollars to the man who can stand three rounds with Mr. Heany. And you'll be interested to know that in over a dozen exhibitions to date, Mr. Heany remains unbeaten and the challenge money is as yet unpaid. So come forward one and all, you men. I hear that the town of, er"—he consulted his scribbled card—"the town of Gilead, Nebraska, boasts some of the finest, brawniest men in the region. Who among you will be the first to challenge our champion for twenty-five dollars?"

As the man talked on, the boxer stood behind him with his arms crossed. He looked like any number of veteran prizefighters Ki had seen, with a wide, flattened face that was a map of scars and lumps. The face had been broken many times, and Ki somehow doubted that Heany was undefeated—else why wouldn't he be heavyweight champion and fighting for more money than a carnival could pay?

The challenge was answered by a fellow who emerged from a group of shouting cowhands. His comrades cheered him up into the ring and hooted derisively at Heany. The cowboy was at least three inches taller than the older fighter, and he quickly shirked his hat, vest, and shirt. The pudgy man in pinstripes advised him to remove his gunbelt also, as well as the items in his pockets. So, clad only in pants and boots, like Heany, the youngster threw up his fists, ready to fight.

The announcer first got his name and called it out: "Mr. Frank Orwell of the Slash D Cattle Corporation! Good luck to you, Mr. Orwell!" The man then stepped out of the ring and stood by a triangular dinner bell suspended from a hook. Holding his pocket watch to his nose, he clanged the start of the first round.

As the contest began, Orwell stood confidently in the middle of the ring, watching the older man circle around him. The ranch hand lifted his fists and beckoned Heany to come at him. But the wily professional kept moving and kept just out of Orwell's reach, silently taunting him, jabbing at the air around him.

The youngster could take this treatment only for so long. His clean face soon betrayed impatience, and he stepped toward Heany. Heany rocked back to avoid a sweeping hook that the kid sent his way. Orwell kept his balance and continued to approach, sending out a left this time that met with Heany's upraised right arm. At least the ranch hand had made contact, and it felt good. Heany kept backing and circling, moving on his toes. For such a heavily muscled man, he moved well, possessing some surprising quickness.

Ki watched intently, trying to gauge the professional fighter's plan. It was clear to him that Heany was in full control of the match. Still, the kid was bigger and perhaps stronger than the Irishman. If he could land that one killing punch, he could walk away with the prize. But Heany must know that too, and he'd use all his skills to stay out of range.

Orwell stayed on the offensive, fronting Heany and peppering the space around his head with jabbing fists. Cannily, the experienced pro seemed to know where the punches were coming from, and he managed to keep his face out of harm's way each time.

The bell ended the round and the men went to opposite corners of the ring for a breather. But before they could catch their breath, the second round had begun. As in the first, Heany toyed with the youngster for the first minute or so. Then, suddenly—or so it seemed—Orwell had the Irishman backed up on the ropes. He connected with a series of body punches as the gathered crowd came to life and started to cheer. His face a mean, grim mask, Heany took the blows and waited for his chance. Orwell got cocky and dropped both hands, intending to pummel the older man into submission right there on the ropes. This was obviously what Heany had been waiting for.

With one stinging left hook, Heany connected with the side of Orwell's face and spun the kid halfway around until he was now crouched in the corner, and Heany was in control. Disoriented, surprised at the quick turnaround, Orwell gaped at his opponent—and Heany had plenty of time to blast the youngster once in the face, splitting open Orwell's right cheek.

Reflexively, Orwell brought his hands up to shield his injured head. Heany used the opportunity to batter the kid's midsection with several fast, hard blows. Furious and startled, the young man unleashed his fists in a flurry of punches that drove Heany back. His chest heaving, Orwell darted out of the corner, the blood on his cheek mingling with a river of sweat.

Ki looked down at Yvonne's face. The girl watched Orwell with fear and sympathy. She, too, knew that his chances were diminishing by the second. Ki returned his attention to the ring just in time to see Heany land a powerful right uppercut beneath Orwell's outthrust jaw.

The youngster was lifted from his feet, but managed to land upright. He shook his head to clear his brain. Heany stepped back, plainly astonished that the kid was still on his feet. Clearly, the Nebraskan was a tough one, and it would take all of the professional's skill to deck him. Warily, Heany circled his stunned opponent, awaiting another opening.

Orwell wasn't about to give up. Now he moved, rather unsteadily, with Heany—keeping the man within arm's length but not wasting futile blows on a moving target. He blocked a roundhouse right and ducked under Heany's fol-

31

lowup left hook. On his way up he stung Heany with a swift, short gut-punch. The local crowd once again roared.

Feinting right, then left, Heany watched Orwell's eyes try to follow him. The kid's face was cut and swollen, and the pro would take advantage of that.

Darting around Orwell in a tight circle, Heany peppered the youngster with quick jabs, hoping to drive his defenses down. But the cowboy stubbornly stood his ground, giving back as best he could. Heany crouched and weaved, avoiding Orwell's fists. He changed directions and the kid staggered to follow him. Heany sneaked a blow inside, grazing his opponent's nose and snapping his head back. For a split second Orwell shut his eyes, wincing with intense pain. This was all Heany needed.

The fighter hauled off and smashed the kid twice, once on each side of the jaw. The ranch hand toppled to the canvas, not knowing what had hit him. The pudgy man in the pinstriped coat hopped into the ring and counted the youngster out. He held Heany's arm in the air and declared him still the undefeated champ.

Murmuring its concern for the downed Orwell, the crowd slowly dispersed. The cowboy's friends carried him away.

Slightly sickened by the brutal boxing match, Yvonne led Ki back to the boardinghouse. She held his hand as they walked slowly through the deserted streets of the town. And as the lights and noise of the carnival show receded behind them, a quiet, urgent tension grew up between them.

The girl said, "I could stay up all night. I'm not tired at all."

"It's late. Mrs. Oxbridge will be worried about you. Besides, I *am* tired."

"She's a nice lady, Mr. Ki, but she doesn't run my life."

"Not 'Mr. Ki,' just Ki," he corrected her. "She is your family. You must respect and obey her."

"Oh, I never disobey her, Ki. She never tells me what

32

to do. She thinks I'm a wild girl. But she loves me, and I love her. Say, how's your arm that got shot? It must hurt awful bad."

"It will heal," was all Ki said.

This girl was an independent one. A lot like Jessie—headstrong and pretty and straightforward in talk and manner. Yvonne exuded a strong, alluring sexuality as well; but he wondered if she knew much about men. For all her frankness, she was still very young, and he doubted that she had ever been properly bedded.

Yvonne stopped and looked up into Ki's eyes. "What are you thinking about?" she asked. "You're always thinking."

Ki laughed gently. "Isn't a man supposed to think?"

"Oh, yes. It's just that I don't know any who do. Not in this town. I can almost hear your mind working. Are you thinking about me?"

"Yes," said Ki. "I am thinking how pretty you are, and how young."

"I'm eighteen—well, almost. I'm a full-grown woman, Ki."

"You have some more growing to do. Not much, it is true."

"But sometimes a girl can't wait—if she feels like a woman and needs what a woman needs. Can you understand that, Ki?"

They were less than a block from the boardinghouse. The girl clung to him, her shadowed eyes pleading for affection. At that moment she did indeed look more like a woman than like a seventeen-year-old girl; and the samurai could not deny his own interest, his own need. It was becoming difficult to control himself, but he tried. He knew that these young fillies, as cowboys called girls, could be fickle; she might not really want to go all the way with him; perhaps she was fooling herself. He wasn't sure.

He said, "Do you know what you want, Yvonne?"

"I want *you*," the girl said, squeezing his hand. "We can go to my room."

They did, treading quietly up the stairs so as not to rouse Mrs. Oxbridge and her boarders. Yvonne locked her door. She did not light a lamp. She led Ki to her bed, where they lay down side by side.

Their first kiss was tentative as they explored the feel and taste of each other. Then Ki began carefully to undress the girl, who lay on the bed, her eyes closed. He unbuttoned her blouse and skirt and pulled them off, then unlaced her boots and dropped them on the floor beside the bed. At first she remained unmoving, as if she were asleep. Then, as he stood over her and peeled off his own shirt, she opened her eyes. She saw the wide shoulders and firm, muscular stomach, the smooth chest, and a surge of passion—unlike anything she had ever known—coursed through her body.

Yvonne wore no corset, no undergarments at all beneath her clothes so she was naked as Ki stepped out of his pants. He stretched out beside her on the bed and held her. "We will make love only if you wish to make love," he told her.

"Ki." She invoked his name as if it were a prayer. "Please love me."

He took her face to his and kissed her. Their lips met in a crushing union, and he parted hers with his tongue. She resisted at first, but finally gave way to his insistent probing. Their tongues mingled warmly, darting and sliding. Her arms wound around his bare back and she held him to her and put her whole heart into the long, intense kiss. Her head spun in confusion and need. Who was this man, after all? Why did she feel so complete in his arms? Why did she want him to stay with her forever in the coolness of her room?

Ki stroked her hair. "You are beautiful, with hair as black as the hair of women from my country, and skin so white."

He cupped her round breast in one hand. She moaned

almost inaudibly. Then he ran his hand over her soft flesh, raking the dark nipple with his long fingers. She emitted a soft cry of delight, her eyes now tightly closed again.

As he explored her body with his sure hands, she relaxed. He felt the soft swell of her stomach and the smooth slenderness of her thighs, then ran his fingers down her leg and around to the firm fullness of her buttocks. She responded by moving against him, slowly at first, then more quickly.

Finally she freed the arm that was pinned beneath him and tentatively reached for his growing erection. When her fingers touched him, he felt a jolt of heat. She wrapped her fingers around the hardness of him and squeezed. He took her nipple between his fingers, pinching softly, and she arched her back slightly, not releasing his erect member. He felt her hand run up and down the length of his shaft, as skillfully as a courtesan's hand. It went on like this for several minutes that seemed an eternity of painful arousal. She held on to his neck with her free hand and pulled his lips to hers yet again. This time she was the aggressor in their hot kiss as her hand held his stiffness.

Ki's hand snaked between her legs, which were clamped together like a virgin's. But as they kissed, she relaxed and parted her thighs slightly, allowing his hand to slide up their smoothness. She gasped as his fingers found the warm, wet place where her legs met. He felt the soft lips and ran his hand up onto the furry mound, and then down again to the inviting region, rubbing the lips, trying to further awaken the animal need in her.

Yvonne cooed at his touch and spread her legs, giving him all the access he wanted to her tingling sex. Still she held on to his jutting sword with all her strength, as if it were made of gold and she'd die if she let it go. Pain and pleasure shot through Ki as she squeezed him harder. He grunted in rough counterpoint to her soft female sighs.

Then he plunged his middle finger into her tight sheath. He pushed it all the way in and she bucked in response.

"Ooooh, Ki," she cried. His finger went in and out and she felt her own lubricating juices flowing heavily. She was starving now for his love, for the touch of this man who came from a faraway place and was taking her into the wild night sky of passion.

She released his shaft and flung both arms around his muscular shoulders, rocking with the motion of his plunging finger. He added another digit, pushing them both into her tightness, and she groaned with anticipation. She opened her eyes to watch his dark, serious face; he pressed against her and she felt his stiff member at her side.

Ki bent his head and kissed her white neck, licking at it. He pulled his fingers from inside her and wrapped his arms around her waist, moving his mouth farther down, over her breasts. He trapped a nipple between his teeth and began sucking and nibbling on it. Her moans grew louder as he toyed with her, stroking with his tongue, teasing with his teeth.

"Ki, Ki," she whispered harshly, struggling to keep from crying out and awakening Mrs. Oxbridge in the next room. Luckily, the older woman slept soundly after a hard day's work.

"Let our spirits talk to each other," he said, barely able to speak himself.

"I can't take it anymore," Yvonne said. She fumbled for his stiff rod and grasped it. Her thumb pressed on the head and she rubbed it around and around. "I want you inside me, Ki. I must have you."

Ki gave her nipple one last flick of the tongue and pushed himself up beside her. Then he lifted himself on top of her and came down gently until their bodies were pressed hotly together, without an inch of space between them.

"Put me inside you," Ki commanded huskily.

Yvonne obeyed, first rubbing the head of his erection against the wet, musky lips of her sex. Then she pushed his member inside, and he was lost in the depths of her.

Slowly he pushed his aching sword all the way in with one thrust, and then retreated, and then was fully inside her sheath, and then out. The tightness enveloped his hot, engorged member. And he jerked almost involuntarily at the exquisite sensation it created. He increased the pace and she lifted her legs and locked them around the small of his back. Her thighs pressed around his muscular hips and her heels dug deeply into his buttocks.

Before he knew it, he was pumping furiously in and out of her, his throbbing rod working its own will on both of them. Her legs tightened around his back and she met his thrusts with a jerky movement of her pelvis, pushing herself up to meet his plunges. Faster and faster they made love, now completely lost in the nether world of wild animal heat. Their bodies were fused and they melted into each other as their climax built and built.

Ki held her to him, conscious only of her long, supple body matching his in warmth and intensity of purpose. Beads of sweat popped out on his forehead and his chest as they worked to give pleasure to each other, as they worked out the primal need they both felt at this awful moment of explosive union.

"Oh, God, oh, God!" she exclaimed. The bed creaked beneath them.

Ki plunged ever more deeply and withdrew almost all the way before thrusting back into her. He uttered a long, low growl as he felt her internal muscles contracting. She was coming now.

"Yes, Ki, yes! Oh, lover!" She was no longer a vulnerable, curious little girl. She was a full-grown woman now, and she felt like only a full-grown woman could—filled up with her man and nothing else in the whole world.

Ki could barely control himself any longer. He plunged hard and fast until the wave of his own climax began to break over him. She bucked like a mustang beneath him, meeting his thrusts with urgent movements of her own. Her contractions milked him greedily, and suddenly he burst.

White-hot flares exploded in his mind as he came, filling her with his seed. Spurt after spurt erupted from his long throbbing sword. It seemed to take forever to stop, as the girl thrashed beneath him and his own excitement spilled itself out of the cup. It was nearly over now. His arms tightly holding her, he finished, collapsing with fatigue on top of the slender girl.

Rarely had Ki spent himself so entirely as with Yvonne. For a while they lay in silent embrace, her quiet contractions slowly fading away and his own manhood growing soft in its warm sheath. Then he withdrew and rolled away from her.

Finally the girl spoke: "Ki, did you—did you like it? Did I do all right?"

"Yes," the samurai replied. There was much more he wanted to tell her about the way of love, but now was not the time.

"I'm so glad!" She snuggled up against his naked, per-spiration-coated body. "But I'm scared too," she added.

"Why are you frightened?"

"Because whoever killed Mr. Kelso—they aren't going to want you and Jessie to find out."

"Do you know anything about how he died?" Ki asked her.

"No," Yvonne said. "I only know I don't want you to die, Ki."

Chapter 3

Early the next morning, Ki met Jessie in her room. Rested
and refreshed, she looked like a new woman. Wearing her
familiar blue denim jeans and a brightly checkered riding
shirt, she sat at the foot of bed, brushing her lustrous hair.
"Did you enjoy the carnival with Yvonne?" she asked when
Ki came in.

The samurai answered in one word: "Interesting."

"Not as interesting as the girl, though."

He knew she was teasing him, but be wouldn't give her
the satisfaction. "She seems to be a very nice young lady."

Jessie's emerald eyes twinkled. "I can see you're not
going to say another word, so I'll quit. She is a nice girl,
though. And she's in love with you."

"How do you know that?"

"Lord, Ki, anyone can see it from the way she looks at

you. Don't play ignorant with me, you wily Japanese," she prodded.

"It is you people of the West who are inscrutable."

She laughed. "Are you as hungry as I am?" She tossed aside her hairbrush.

"I am reminded of a proverb: 'When the belly speaks, the mind must listen.'"

"How wise you are," Jessie said with a grin. "Let's get some breakfast."

Before they left, Jessie inspected Ki's injured arm and changed the dressing. The wound was healing nicely. They ate a quick meal downstairs in the restaurant off the lobby of the hotel and went out into the already-hot street. The day promised to be a scorcher. The town, though, was going about business as usual. The main avenue was clogged with horse and wagon traffic as well as people hurrying to and fro from shops and offices.

In fact, Gilead gave the appearance of a prosperous, up-and-coming city, with a growing cattle business in the surrounding county, along with profitable farms and local businesses. The Starbuck operation had, until now, played a small but important part in the community's economic affairs, importing as it did everything from chinaware and watches to Mexican saddles and English firearms. It wasn't enough to make Dudley Kelso, or the company, rich; but it had provided Kelso a decent living and brought products from the outside world to this burgeoning Nebraska town. His main customers had been housewives who wanted to give their homes a touch of opulence and working men who were eager to spend some of their money on small luxuries. Such folks were out this morning, doing their banking or shopping or selling their goods in the stores. All in all, Gilead appeared a rather impressive, energetic town.

At the office, Jessie and Ki found Mrs. Oxbridge bustling about, busying herself with a dustcloth, pretending that there was much more work for her than there actually was. She looked up from polishing a lamp when the pair came in.

"Good morning, Miss Starbuck, Mr. Ki." She dropped the cloth into one of the voluminous pockets of her apron. "Sleep well last night?"

"What are you doing here, Mrs. Oxbridge?" asked Jessie. "You didn't have to come in today. And the boarding-house—surely you have work there."

"Yvonne can take care of that place. This place is—well, it's in dire need of a good scrubbing."

Jessie shook her head in amusement. She liked and in-stinctively trusted this big, busy woman.

"I can brew up some coffee, ma'am," said Mrs. Ox-bridge.

"I'd like that," Jessie acknowledged. "Please bring it into Mr. Kelso's office. I'm going to read over his papers." Ki followed her into the office.

As she had done the day before, Jessie looked over Kel-so's notes and correspondence. She discovered that he had been involved in several schemes to expand the company's operations in the area, including an ingenious mail-order plan. Sensing that there were a lot of potential customers all over the state of Nebraska, he wanted to make Starbuck imports and other products available to them without their having to travel to Gilead.

Also, Jessie found a draft of a letter addressed to her at the Circle Star ranch, requesting permission to begin the mail-order operation and outlining his plans. He would need, he suggested, a thousand dollars from the company to launch the new business, and he figured on being able to recoup that amount within the first six to twelve months; everything after that would be profit.

As she read these materials, she found herself wondering what kind of man Kelso really was. There was no question but that he had intelligence and drive and ambition, and he seemed from these papers, and from Mrs. Oxbridge's ac-

41

count, to have been an honest, hardworking man with the qualities of a scholar and an inventor. And the more she saw of his skills, the more she realized that others could see him in a different light—as a threat to their interests. With the mysterious "discovery" in Beacon, with the plans for a mail-order business, with Kelso's ability to turn ideas into reality, he could present some fierce competition to the established business community....

As if in answer to her thoughts, Mrs. Oxbridge appeared at the door. The woman looked from Ki, who stood quietly by the desk reading over Jessie's shoulder, to Jessie. "There are some gentlemen here to see you, Miss." The way she said *gentlemen* left no doubt that the species in question were anything but.

"Mr. Ki, you better come too," she added meaningfully.

Stepping quietly behind Jessie, Ki went with her into the outer room, his mind alert to potential danger, his body poised for action.

Four men were in the room. The air was thick with unfriendliness as Jessie and Ki looked from one man's face to another. One of the men was Sheriff Bob Lowell. The others were strangers. Mrs. Oxbridge glared at the men, making no bones about her distrust. But the men ignored the plump woman, giving their full attention to Jessie and her Oriental companion.

"Miss Starbuck, my name is Wallace Winslow." The man, larger and heavier and better dressed than the others, was obviously the leader. In fact, Winslow looked as if he could wrestle a bull and stand a chance of winning. His tremendous bulk was mostly muscle, with very little flab hanging on his arms or around his gut. He was very tall, as well, and probably weighed over two hundred fifty pounds, and he wore a well-cut black suit, a black vest, and a clean white shirt. A sparkling gold watch chain hung across his midsection. He did not remove his stylish black felt hat, nor did he wear a gun. Jessie, however, guessed he knew how to handle one; she figured that before he'd made enough money to hire other men's guns, there had been a time when his own skill with weaponry made him a man to be reckoned with. There was still a gleam of violence in his eyes, and a ready swing to his big hands. But time had slowed him somewhat, and he moved with a bulky grace and spoke in a measured, raspy tone of voice.

Winslow extended his hand, which sported a big diamond ring. Despite her immediate distrust of Winslow—the name Sheriff Lowell had mentioned last night—Jessie shook his proffered hand. His grip was powerful, though he didn't try to squeeze her hand to a pulp, as some men did. Then he introduced the others.

Lamar Mohart was the oldest of the group, a white-bearded, quiet-looking man with light blue eyes that bored into Jessie's. He was the chief local banker, and his pale skin and white hands were evidence of the endless days he spent ciphering in his ledgers and counting money. He merely nodded to Jessie in silent, superior acknowledgment.

Next was Sam Bearinger who, said Winslow, owned Gilead's largest general mercantile store. The merchant was stocky, of average height, with a shock of thick brown hair. Wearing a less expensive suit than his two peers, he gave the impression of recently acquired prosperity, and there was a glint of triumph in his dark eyes. He smiled and tipped his hat to Jessie and Ki. Of the three, he looked the most out of place—as if he wanted to be back behind the counter in his store, making money and friends.

"And you've already met Sheriff Lowell, our esteemed law enforcer in Box Butte County."

Lowell did not meet Jessie's gaze, but sort of half-lifted his hand and dropped it again. His face was mottled pink and white, and he stood there unsteadily behind the other three.

"The sheriff informs me that you are inquiring into the unfortunate circumstances of Mr. Kelso's death. I must tell you that we—all of us here—were shocked and saddened by the murder. But the killers left no evidence, nothing for Sheriff Lowell to go on in his search for them."

"You say *killers,* Mr. Winslow," Jessie retorted. "How do you know there was more than one?"

She didn't like the first impression she was getting of Winslow; he was very transparently telling her to call off the dogs, to trust the alcoholic lawman to do his job. But Lowell was the last one in the world she'd trust to investigate Kelso's killing—because there was no question in her mind now that he was controlled by these men, the vested interests in Gilead. And she was beginning to believe they wanted the incident swept under the carpet for their own purposes—whatever they may have been.

"This is a good town, Miss Starbuck—a decent town. The sheriff's working hard to clean out the bad element, aren't you, Bob?"

The ineffectual lawman gave an alcoholic grunt, raising his unsure eyes for a second, then dropping them.

"The cattlemen bring a lot of business, and a lot of trouble too. We're cutting down on the trouble, though. My thinking is that old Kelso got himself hoo-rawed and the cowboys went a step too far. Of course, they cleaned him out—loose cash and such. And we're all sorry about that. Kelso was a good man."

"I appreciate your sympathy," Jessie said. "But I don't think it was just some drunk trail hands out for a good time."

"Oh?" Winslow's thick, dark eyebrows rose to emphasize his query. "And how do you suppose it happened?"

"It wasn't a robbery. At least that wasn't the main reason they killed him." She said it without expression, without giving any hint as to who, if anyone, she suspected of having Kelso killed. She was testing Winslow; and the burly businessman saw it.

"I admire your candor—and your loyalty to a dead em-

44

ployee. However, I think you'll find that the sheriff here carried out a thorough investigation and came to the only possible conclusion."

Behind Winslow, the gray-faced sheriff kept his eyes glued to the floor. No matter what the big man said, this law officer did not inspire the least bit of confidence.

"Are you in town for long?" Winslow asked, changing the subject. "If so, I'd like to extend you an invitation to stay at my hotel, the Nebraska House, which by all accounts is the most comfortable hostelry in Gilead. Isn't that right, Sam?"

"Sure, Mr. Winslow," Bearinger said.

Jessie said, "Ki and I are already registered at another place."

"It should be simple enough to have my people remove your belongings to the Nebraska. And I'm prepared to offer you free accommodations, as a gesture of our good faith."

As a bribe, more likely, Jessie thought. She said, "No thank you."

Winslow's thick eyebrows came together as he frowned. He was not accustomed to being refused. "But there's no finer hotel, as I said," he went on.

"And I said no thank you. Now is that all you wanted to see me about? Surely you all did not come here to offer me excuses and condolences on Mr. Kelso's passing."

"We're all very busy men, Miss Starbuck," said Winslow, a note of impatience in his harsh basso voice. "We wouldn't have come just for that, no. We came to discuss a business proposition."

"What sort of proposition?" she asked, stealing a sidelong glance at Ki.

Ki stood with his arms crossed over his chest, straight-backed and as still as a statue. He was studying these men, watching their every move and listening to their every word. And he was prepared to break an arm or a leg if one of them made a move against Jessie. But judging from the looks of them, they were not here to cause her physical harm.

"It is very simple," said Mohart, the banker, in a quiet, croaking voice. "We wish to buy this office—now that Mr. Kelso is no longer here to carry on. We assume that you wish to close your operation here in Gilead."

"I intend no such thing," Jessie shot back. "In heaven's name, what makes you think I want to sell you anything?"

"We are prepared to offer a substantial settlement," Mohart said, unmoved by her startled reaction. "Surely you realize that Kelso was driving this office into bankruptcy?"

"Why do you say that, Mr. Mohart? I've seen the books. I have no reason to believe that he was failing to make money, and he was planning to make more by expanding his business."

"Poor man. He must have felt he had to conceal it from you. He made it plain to me, at any rate, that he was in deep trouble," said Winslow. "And to Mr. Mohart here. Isn't that right, Lamar?"

The banker mumbled his assent. He looked to be a mean-hearted man, and impatient with the whole business. He eyed the office with keen greed—probably already adding up the rent they could charge for it, once Jessie let them have it.

"You see, Miss Starbuck," Winslow continued, "Kelso extended himself too far. He had what he called ideas. You and I would call them follies."

"Speak for yourself," Jessie said, anger boiling up within her at the big man's superior attitude. And she did not believe a word of his story that Kelso was going broke. "What proof do you have of your claim?" she asked defiantly.

Winslow tilted his massive head at her, as if he were having trouble hearing. But he kept smiling condescendingly. "My dear Miss Starbuck, you have our word as gentlemen. I'm sure you'll find nothing on paper. Kelso was too clever and too desperate for that. If you care to look at Mr. Mohart's books, you'll see that Kelso had borrowed heavily, especially over the past year. We always assumed that he had your blessing for these adventures of his, that he was doing it for your company. But as it turns out, his schemes threatened both your company and our interests."

"How could he be a threat to you?"

Winslow's pale eyes went ice-cold as he explained. "Your man had the gall to try to set up a mail-order business to offer sundry goods to folks all over the county and the state. He did not realize that such a business would cut into Mr. Bearinger's store for instance. Or that it would reduce the number of people traveling to Gilead to do their buying and conduct other business."

"And reduce *your* customers," Jessie said, realizing that Winslow had a personal ax to grind, along with his professed concern for the community.

"Yes," admitted the hotel owner. "And there would have been other businessmen affected as well. So you see, mine is not a totally selfish position."

"But what about the people who'd be able to buy more goods, more cheaply? Did you ever consider their interests?"

"That is not the way a good businessman thinks, Miss Starbuck," Winslow said. "That is not the way to maximize profit."

Jessie remained silent for a moment. She wondered if she should bring up the issue of Kelso's "discovery" in Beacon. Did these men know anything about it? Somehow, she doubted there was anything Kelso was involved in that they did not know. But Winslow had mentioned nothing of it. Did that mean it was unimportant to him? Or that it was *very* important?

"Whatever you want to offer me, I'll consider," she said diplomatically. "But I'm not going to sell immediately. You'll understand if I take my time and think about it."

"Time is like money," Winslow observed. "There is too often not enough of either."

"I'll remember that, Mr. Winslow," she said.

Winslow stood there, bulking large in his black suit, his fierce demeanor promising nothing but trouble if she didn't go along with him. Bearinger, Mohart, and Lowell backed him quietly—but they were there as testimony to his deep-running influence in Gilead.

"Does this mean you intend to keep this office in business?" he demanded.

"I might."

"Without someone to run it?" Winslow prodded. "Or are you going to manage it yourself?"

"I might," Jessie repeated, giving no quarter.

Winslow glanced at Mrs. Oxbridge and Ki. He caught the Oriental staring straight at him, and looked away. "You're new in Gilead, Miss Starbuck," Winslow said. "You don't know how things work around here. I'm sure you'll find out quickly enough, though. And you may regret your stubbornness."

"Is that a threat?" she blazed. She'd had quite enough of Winslow's not-so-subtle bullying.

"Not at all," said the burly hotel owner, backing off a bit at this display of the famous Starbuck temper.

Lowell tried to burp quietly, but in the stillness of the room it echoed. Mrs. Oxbridge wiped her hands on her apron and looked away, visibly disgusted. It was an appropriate signal that this discussion was over. Winslow and the others took their leave, filing out the front door one by one. Winslow, of course, was last, and he had the last word. "We'll continue this matter later, perhaps under friendlier circumstances, Miss Starbuck. Good day."

By late afternoon, Jessie and Ki had gone over every bill, every letter, every book and ledger, every scrap in Kelso's office. There was no evidence of any financial problems

48

with the operation, and no evidence of any wrongdoing on Kelso's part. What they did find were some more details on the mysterious development in Beacon.

"Ki, come look at his," Jessie said, sitting at the cluttered desk with a small map spread out before her.

He came to her side and studied the map with her. Although the locations on the map were not labeled, it struck him immediately what it signified. "This is the area outside the town called Beacon," he said. "Your man Kelso probably drew it himself. He was a man of many talents."

"And see these marks here and here," Jessie said. "These must indicate the spots where he thought he'd find oil—or whatever he was looking for."

"Jessie," said Ki, "do you think Winslow knows about this?"

"Even though he didn't say anything about it, I can't help thinking he does know. There's a lot more potential in oil than in a little mail-order business. I hear that even though prices are low right now, folks down in the Indian Territory are making money because the stuff is in plentiful supply; they bring up hundreds of barrels a day. One fellow down there even had the bright idea of bringing in tank cars on a spur line so he could just pump it into the car and ship it out by train."

"But has anyone discovered oil in Nebraska before this?"

"No. And I don't think there could be much up here—except maybe isolated fields."

"Like Beacon."

"Look at this here." Jessie held up a letter from a man in that town—a fellow named Dale Knowlton. "Apparently Kelso was working with this Knowlton, a blacksmith by trade. Knowlton was going to build a drill, and he'd already ordered the equipment. They were supposed to meet tomorrow to talk about starting the project. I ought to talk to Knowlton."

"And we must see what this place called Beacon is like.

Tonight we rest. Tomorrow we ride."

Jessie sat back in the chair, exhaustion and worry scoring her beautiful face. "No telling what Winslow and his boys will do in our absence. Damn, I wish I knew what Winslow is planning—and if he has even an inkling of this Beacon discovery. I just can't buy that bullshit about the mail-order business threatening them all, and Kelso's begging for money from Mohart."

Ki straightened to his full height and smiled, his strong white teeth gleaming. "You talk sometimes like a cowboy. Where did you learn such language?"

"From the ranch hands at the Circle Star Ranch. Where else?" She, smiled too. "My father would wash my mouth out with soap if he could hear me talk sometimes. I usually had sense enough to speak properly around him. If you recall, though, he could cuss a blue streak when he had a mind to."

The memory of her father was never far from Jessie's mind. At times it was as if he were not dead at all, as if the assassins' bullets had somehow miraculously not shredded his powerful body. For Alex Starbuck's presence was with her wherever she went, the force of his personality stamped on whatever she did. It was not an oppressive feeling, but a painful one. Jessie longed for his comforting hug; she ached to hear him speak words of guidance and reassurance. But he was gone forever. And she had vowed, on the day he died, to avenge his cruel death. That vow kept her company as her father now could not.

As angry as she got at men like Winslow, she remained angrier still at the cartel that had killed her father: a group of foreign businessmen who were fearful and jealous of Alex Starbuck's spectacular success in the Far East. Single-handedly, Starbuck had carved out an empire. No one man could match his skill in forging profitable ties with the Japanese to import precious goods to the United States. No one man could challenge his drive and business acumen in consolidating such disparate interests as mining, imports, and cattle all over the West. No one man could stand up to Starbuck—but when his enemies banded together in a secret alliance and sent hired guns to finish him, Alex Starbuck could not stand up to the hail of bullets that cut him down in the prime of life.

And years before, when Jessie was a child too young to remember it, those same faceless enemies had engineered the death of her mother, staging an accident in Europe that killed the beautiful, spirited woman and left Starbuck and his daughter alone in the world. How hard Alex Starbuck had worked to raise Jessie properly! Yes, he had spoiled her; yes, she had had the best of everything; yes, she had grown up on the rich Circle Star ranch in Texas with the wind in her hair and the sun on her face. Slowly, painfully, Alex Starbuck had conquered his grief and invested all of his love in the shining-eyed girl. He had educated her, taught her to ride and shoot as well as any boy, and given her a sense of self-worth that no one could ever take away from her.

Now Jessie had only Ki, her father's most trusted friend. And she had the written records of Alex Starbuck's tumultuous life, including his meticulously kept diary—wherein he recorded everything he knew about the hated cartel: names, dates, companies, transactions. He had been determined to know his enemy; and he left Jessie with a helpful tool in her quest for vengeance. For if she encountered a man who was named in that diary as an agent of the cartel, that man was as good as dead.

It meant living with death every day, and being ready to die herself—expecting sudden death as certainly as other people expected bad weather, as a fact of life. But Alex Starbuck would be avenged. Jessie knew that what she was doing would have made him proud of her. That was what she lived for; and if necessary, that was what she would die for.

51

Through the grimy windows of Kelso's office the late sun slanted in yellow bars. Mrs. Oxbridge had gone home to prepare supper for the house, and all was quiet as Jessie and Ki quietly wondered how it all added together—and if the cartel was somehow connected in this business. Jessie folded the map of Beacon and the letter for Dale Knowlton and stuffed them into the pocket of her vest.

As they were leaving the Starbuck office, a messenger boy met them. He had a note for Jessie. He stood by, waiting for a reply.

Jessie read it and passed it to Ki. It was from Winslow.

My dear Miss Starbuck,

I would be honored if you would consent to join me for dinner this evening at my suite in the Nebraska House at eight o'clock.

There are further matters I should like to discuss with you concerning the disposition of the Starbuck office in Gilead.

The boy will convey your reply. I remain

Your servant,
Wallace Winslow.

"What do you think, Ki?"

"I think I should be there with you. This man is not playing straight, as you Americans say."

"But the invitation is for me alone." She winked. "I'm interested in hearing what he has to say."

"It's up to you, Jessie. But I advise you to be very careful."

"As always, I value your advice, Ki." She turned to the messenger, a ten year old with a dirt-smudged face. "Tell Mr. Winslow that I will be there at eight. And thank him for his kind invitation."

The boy scrambled away toward the hotel. Jessie locked the office door and stepped out onto the boardwalk. Briefly she entertained second thoughts, then shrugged them away. She'd give Winslow a fair audience—and she'd do her damnedest to find out from him just how much he knew about Kelso's plan to drill outside Beacon—and if those plans had anything to do with the man's death.

Chapter 4

Julius Goodpaster was writing a letter at his desk in the custom-built wagon that was almost as long as a railroad car. The interior was lit with a pair of clean-burning lamps on a polished mahogany fold-down slab that served as a dining table. The walls of the wagon were lined with a plush light beige fabric that partially reflected the glowing light and gave the space an airy look and feeling, even in the gathering darkness outside. There was plenty of room, more than enough for an average-sized man to stand and move around easily. Along the back wall of the wagon, behind the desk, there was a soft couch extending a good seven feet. And since Goodpaster was larger than average-sized, the couch where he slept was the best place to stretch out full length.

He scribbled on the paper with a steel-nibbed pen, dipping it in a large, black-stained inkwell. He kept writing as a man entered the wagon without knocking.

"Sit down, Steel Knife," Goodpaster said. The man, a lanky half-breed with long black hair, sat down and waited. Goodpaster blotted the letter, folded it, and put it in an envelope. He addressed it with the single word *Winslow*.

"I want you to ride into town with me, Steel Knife. You're to deliver this letter. I have business with the sheriff."

"Yes, boss."

"And rustle me up a spare revolver. Meet me back here in fifteen minutes."

The half-breed went out. Goodpaster sat back in his leather-covered chair and lit a ready-made cigarette that he took from a lacquered box. The blue smoke curled up from his nostrils as he exhaled.

In his black and gold checkered vest, high white collar, and silk tie, he looked the part of a successful carnival owner. His blunt features were somehow handsome, and his face was framed by thick, wavy brown hair and long brown sideburns. He puffed on his cigarette as he considered the current state of affairs. It wasn't time to panic—far from it. But that blasted Darrel was in jail, and the girl and her Oriental companion were asking too many questions. It wasn't as neat as he had planned it. Still, no cause for alarm. The fight in Beacon would come off two days from now, and that would solve his major problem—acquisition of the land he wanted.

The two pieces of the puzzle that weren't fitting right, however, were Darrel and Winslow. He didn't trust the self-important hotel owner and must remind him who was running the show. As for Darrel, it wasn't a question of trust—the would-be badman was too dumb to betray him—but of putting him to best use. And that required getting him out of jail.

The half-breed returned with the revolver. The two men

then went out to their horses. Goodpaster was camped a mile outside of Gilead, where his carnival show was playing two nights. Last night had been a success, netting nearly five hundred dollars. He hoped, though, that the good folks of Gilead hadn't begun to suffer any ill effects from Dr. Keith's miracle tonic. That had closed the show early several times before. Two nights was the outside limit for a carnival in any small town. Tomorrow the show would go to Beacon, the godforsaken little hamlet that was willing to gamble its soul away for cash money.

Goodpaster and Steel Knife split up at the town limits, the half-breed going to the Nebraska House, the carnival master heading for the jailhouse. When he got there he found Sheriff Bob Lowell and a deputy playing cards. There was a half-empty bottle between them and the place stank of liquor fumes.

Lowell stood up rather unsteadily, his eyes glazed and barely focused. "What can I do for you?" he asked thickly.

Goodpaster said, "I'd like to talk to you alone."

"Kid, take a walk around town—patrol, that is. See what's cooking, eh? Me and this gen'leman has business to talk. Git on out." He waved his hand imperiously, if shakily. The deputy did as he was told—this being his first night on the job.

"I'm Julius Goodpaster. I take it you're Sheriff Lowell."

"Yep. Mighty pleasured to meet you, Mr. Goodpaster. Care for a drink?"

"Thank you, I believe I will." The two men sat down and Lowell poured two drinks. Goodpaster sampled his; it was rotgut, tasted like snake oil. "I came to talk to you about a prisoner you're holding, a Mr. Darrel Kinchloe."

"You mean Darrel? Hell, I didn't know he had a last name."

"He likes just plain Darrel. All the boys call him that. You see, Darrel is an employee—rather, a former employee of mine."

"He works for you?" The lawman squinted at Goodpaster. He was totally confused so far, so he poured himself another shot and gulped it down. That cleared his head some.

"*Former* employee. I don't tolerate rough behavior like his. I understand he caused some trouble for that lady and her companion last night."

"Yeah, he and some other joker who's dead. That gal and her Chinaman brung Darrel in for questioning. He was pretty much out of it, though. China boy beat him up pretty good."

"I'd like to arrange for his bail," Goodpaster said, reaching for his money purse.

"You say bail?" Lowell scratched his head, scattering flakes of dandruff over his shoulders. "I don't rightly recollect—I never said nothin' 'bout no bail. Ain't been no judge 'round, either. Circuit man comes on the fifteenth of the month or thereabouts."

"Let's call this a private arrangement, Sheriff Lowell. Between us. Surely you have the authority to set bail in extraordinary circumstances."

The lawman screwed up his face. "How come you got such an in'erest in this here Darrel if'n he don't work for you no more?"

Goodpaster put down his drink. "Sheriff, I'm trying to do you a favor and you're opposing me every step of the way with unimportant questions."

"They ain't um-portant to me. Darrel and his buddy pretty near tore up Miss Starbuck's place. I cain't just let him go."

"I'm not asking you to free him without taking the proper steps—such as setting a reasonable bail."

"I don't have no idee what would be reasonable bail." Lowell stared into his whiskey glass. His hand was gripped so tightly around the glass that his knuckles were white.

"Would you entertain a suggestion? I'm no expert either,

but we're both reasonable men."

"I reckon so," said Lowell.

"Since this man has proved a danger to your fine community, I think five hundred dollars and a promise that he'll be taken far from here would suffice. Do you agree?"

The sheriff's eyes glowed red. Five hundred dollars! Hell, that was more than he earned in a year, enough maybe to live on for the rest of his life—and he could quit this miserable lawman business for good. Five hundred dollars! Enough to keep him in whiskey for a good long time. He gulped. "Reckon five hunnerd dollars might just do it. Long as yer sure it's legal, that is. Cain't have the sheriff of Box Butte County doin' nothin' ain't legal and proper."

"I assure you, Sheriff Lowell, this arrangement would meet with the approval of any judge and jury. All I'm interested in here is justice, as you are."

"Sure, that makes sense."

"I happen to have the correct amount in cash," said Goodpaster, counting out greenbacks on the table. "Please fetch the prisoner to me, Sheriff, and we'll be on our way."

Jessie had accepted Winslow's invitation, but not without realizing that there were hidden motives for it. Just what those motives were, she aimed to find out.

She wore a low-cut green gown she had purchased at the last minute in a local dress shop. It was part of the game. He would make a play for her, she figured. And she wanted to be ready. There were risks, of course, but she had measured them and decided to go ahead. She would be careful, though, to glean as much useful information from Winslow as she could—without allowing him to get what *he* wanted.

The desk captain at the Nebraska House greeted her obsequiously and led her upstairs to his employer's suite. Knocking on the tall oak door with a gloved hand, the captain stood aside. Winslow himself opened the door. He

59

dismissed the captain and smiled at Jessie.

"Please, Miss Starbuck, come in. Would you care for a drink?"

Her eyes swept over the room. Large, sumptuously furnished, with a small crystal chandelier hanging overhead, and another, larger one over a gleaming teakwood table. There was a marble fireplace at one end of the room, where he guided her with a large hand clamped over her arm. She saw that there were other rooms, accessible through two doors to her right. Jessie was propelled to a satin couch. She sat as he poured her a tall drink.

"You've cultivated a taste for Scotch whiskey, I hope. That is all I drink. I have it imported specially. Which is not easy from a remote Nebraska town. But I do it because I enjoy it."

"There's no better reason to do anything," said Jessie. Winslow was turning on the charm tonight. And it was easy to guess why. She would play along for a while, and keep him at arm's length.

"Spoken like a true lady," he rejoined, raising his glass to her.

Jessie took a careful sip, half suspecting that the drink was drugged. But she tasted the rich liquor and could detect no foreign substance. She remembered that her father often drank Scotch whiskey with his friends. At that point the similarity between Winslow and Alex Starbuck diminished. The man who sat next to her now was a liar and a cheat—and possibly an accessory to murder.

"So tell me, Mr. Winslow," she began bluntly. "Why did you invite me here? It can't be just to get me drunk."

Winslow's broad shoulders rocked with laughter. "You are direct," he declared. "You can't believe that it is the same reason—enjoyment? I enjoy the company of beautiful young women, especially if we have common business interests." He was dressed in a dark blue suit and shiny black boots. Jeweled studs buttoned his shirt and fastened his cuffs. And he still wore the same diamond ring on his right hand. His face was rugged and fleshy at the same time, and he knew how to make his powerful presence weight his words.

"I assumed, as your invitation indicated, that you wanted to continue our earlier conversation. About Ki and me leaving Gilead and selling the Starbuck office to you and your friends. Why am I a threat to you?" Her eyes, nearly the same color as her dress, bored steadily into his. She hoped to force his hand.

"Can't we put business aside for right now?" he said. "I'll have supper sent up. You must be hungry after such a long day."

"I appreciate your hospitality, Mr. Winslow. I would prefer frank talk and another drink before we have supper."

"Call me Wallace. If I may call you Jessie?" He rose and took her glass. "Let's try to be friends."

"Why should I want to be your friend?" she asked, giving no ground.

"Dear girl, perhaps we could establish a relationship that will bring us mutual profit. As I thought about it after our first meeting, it occurred to me that my friends and I might have acted a bit precipitously today. I have no intention of hurting you or of driving you out of business." He poured more whiskey and brought it to her.

"You could have fooled me," she said with a slight smile. Despite his decidedly friendly demeanor, she knew she must not trust him. His ends hadn't changed, but maybe his means had.

"You have a marvelous sense of humor, Jessie. That's rare in a woman."

"Not so rare in the women I know, Mr. Winslow." She took a sip of her second drink. She would have to be careful with the potent liquor. Already she felt somewhat light-headed from the first one. And she wasn't sure where this conversation was leading.

61

"Then I've been associating with the wrong kind," he said.

"Your private life has little bearing on the subject at hand," Jessie said.

"Very well, I'll come straight to the point. Your office here is unwanted competition for the merchants in town. For a long time the people in Gilead, and farmers and cattlemen in the county who come into town to do their business, bought in our shops and stayed in my hotel. It has been a thriving town, and no one willing to work has gone without necessities; we all pull together. That's the way it works. But your man Kelso wanted to change all that with his mail-order merchandise business. He was clearly stepping out of bounds."

"So you had him murdered," Jessie said flatly.

"No, I did not!" Winslow thundered. "I don't know who killed the man."

"What about the two men who attacked us last night in Kelso's office? You know nothing of them? They didn't come from nowhere."

"I tell you I had nothing to do with that. I do not use such tactics to get what I want. In my experience I have found that a few dollars appropriately applied does more than half a dozen hired guns threatening people."

"You've never used guns to get what you want?"

Winslow laughed, a deep gravelly chuckle. "I cannot say 'never.' As a younger man I sometimes resorted to methods which I abhor today." He sat beside her on the sofa, his intimidating bulk as close as she could allow. "You must take my word that I have had no hand in the violence."

A soft rapping at the door brought Winslow to his feet. Relieved, Jessie watched him go to the door. Try as she might, she could not fully believe this man. There was too much at stake here—and Winslow did not impress her as the type of man who would forego any method to get what he wanted, not even killing. But what if he was telling the truth? There was that outside chance. And if not Winslow, then who had ordered Kelso's killing? Who had sent the dogs after Ki and herself last night?

The white-gloved hotel captain handed Winslow a letter. The big man dismissed him and opened the letter. As he read it, his face colored and he muttered a curse under his breath. He stuffed the letter in his pocket and went to fix himself another drink. Although he apparently had a great capacity for liquor, he wouldn't be on his feet long if he kept guzzling it like this. He rejoined Jessie, offering her a perfumed French cigarette from a small box. She declined.

"I don't smoke 'em myself," said Winslow, lighting a long black cigar. "But I know some ladies that do."

"Mr. Winslow, how can I make it any clearer that I'm not like the so-called ladies you know?" She was testing him, exploring the range and limit of his temper. She wanted to know how this man worked; and she wanted to know what was in that letter he had just received. If he was going to be her enemy—which was, she thought, unavoidable— she must know how to fight him.

But the hotel owner remained unruffled. He puffed on his cigar and smiled. "I won't take offense at that, Jessie. I wish you'd call me Wallace. You see, I want to be your friend. We could make ourselves a nice piece of money working together. I assume you plan to follow up on Kelso's discovery at Beacon, and I'd like to join you. I am prepared to invest substantial capital in the venture."

What the hell is going on now? she wondered. *So he does know about it, or at least has an inkling that something is afoot.* She couldn't hold it in any longer. "What do you know about Mr. Kelso's discovery? And how did you find out? Is that why you wanted him out of the way?" Her emerald eyes sparkled with anger. The nerve of this pompous man! What wasn't he telling her? He was playing some sort of confounded game, and she didn't like it.

"It would do neither of us any good to tip our hands,"

Winslow purred. A wide smile crossed his dark face as he went to pour yet another drink. "Suffice it to say I am well aware of what awaits us in Beacon if we move swiftly and decisively. In a word—a potential fortune. And I'd much rather work with the great Starbuck empire than against it."

"Did Kelso tell you these things?"

"Not in so many words. The man enjoyed his whiskey. Sometimes he talked more than was good for him."

"So once you found out, you had him killed," Jessie pursued. "To put him out of the way."

"Nothing so crude, I assure you." The big man replaced himself beside her on the soft sofa. The smoke from his cigar made the air thick. "In fact, we made plans, he and I. In exchange for his abandoning this insane mail-order scheme, I offered him working capital. He hadn't yet agreed to do it—but he would have. He would have seen that it was more sensible. As, I trust, you will too."

"I don't believe a damned word you say." Not only was Winslow now contradicting himself—but he was telling her more than he should. All lies, yes; but how the hell did he know about Beacon? Her mind strained to make the connection. She was more anxious than ever to have a peek at that letter he had just received. Perhaps that held the answer. Certainly he was acting mighty strangely. He was getting drunk, letting his guard down, spouting inane lies.

Obviously pretending to be offended, Winslow said, "Never in twenty years of business transactions has anyone ever called me a liar, Miss Starbuck—Jessie. I make the offer in good faith, and you insist on calling my character into question."

"What about your friends Mohart and Bearinger? Are you including them in this offer? Or are you ready to drop them before they take their cut of the pie?"

"What they don't know certainly cannot hurt them. They'll make out all right."

Jessie fingered the small locket she wore on a thin gold

chain around her neck. Inside was a tiny capsule that she had never, until now, had the occasion to use. Concocted by Myobu, the faithful Japanese servant who had helped raise her and taught her the ways of men and women, the powder in the capsule was a powerful sleeping potion. Men often used this substance to drug and seduce women. Jessie was about to turn the tables.

Winslow was feeling his liquor. He must have been drinking before she arrived. "Aren't you hungry, girl?" he asked. Jessie demurred, saying she'd prefer another drink. "Well, I like that in a woman. I better be careful that you don't drink me under the table. Never live that one down."

"Let me get it," said Jessie. "I'll freshen yours too."

Winslow was only too happy to have the young woman help herself. With her back to her host, Jessie poured the drinks. She slipped the capsule from the locket and dropped it into his glass, watching it dissolve into invisibility. Winslow took an immediate gulp of the Scotch whiskey. Jessie brought her own glass to her lips but did not drink; she'd had more than enough already.

"How come you haven't married?" Winslow asked volubly. "A pretty girl like you, and rich to boot. Seems there would be any number of men . . . any number to snatch you up . . . damn . . ." He swallowed more whiskey. "Better get some food in my stomach—feel strange, tired. Be a good girl . . . call the captain and . . ." Winslow's glass fell onto the carpet, the golden liquor spilling out. He collapsed onto the sofa and began to snore.

Jessie wasted no time in grabbing the letter from his coat pocket. She read it, but did not fully understand what it meant.

After supper at Mrs. Oxbridge's boardinghouse, Ki went out to clear his mind and to put some distance between himself and Yvonne. She would want him to come to her again tonight, but he questioned the wisdom of that. The girl remained in his head, distracting his thoughts. Her lithe body under his, her love cries as he penetrated her, the thin sheen of perspiration on her skin as she moved in rhythm with his thrusts—she was a woman all right. But something else was trying to enter his brain: a warning signal. Ki recognized the feeling and tried to put the image of the girl out of his head.

It was well past sundown as he headed for the jailhouse on Pine Street. Carrying only his sheathed *ko-dachi*, and some *shuriken* in his vest pocket, he moved silently, almost invisibly across the street. What was happening? He wondered if Jessie was safe with Winslow, alone in his hotel suite. She could take care of herself, but still—the man might try something she could not defend herself against.

Then it struck him. Instinctively he changed course and headed for the Starbuck office. Gilead lay under a shroud of darkness. His slipper-shod feet treading noiselessly along the dirt of the street, Ki glanced alertly all around him for signs of activity. He saw none. All the townspeople were probably at the carnival show at the other end of town. The houses and shops in this section were closed. Even the saloon he passed was shuttered for the night.

As he approached the Starbuck office, there were no outward signs of trouble. Ki felt a momentary relief, but he remained cautious. His hand on the *ko-dachi* handle, the Oriental stepped into the alley that sided the building. Cat-like, he slipped down the length of the alley, his eyes and ears open to detect the slightest sound or movement. As he reached the back of the building, the sense of danger in his gut increased. Something was wrong. He stopped. Then he knew.

He smelled smoke. It was almost imperceptible—to anyone but him. Yet he was sure. It was smoke.

Hugging the wall, he edged forward until he could see around the end of the building. There was no one in sight.

He crept to the back window and peered inside. He looked into Kelso's office. All was dark, but the odor of smoke came to him stronger than ever. He tried the window; it was locked. Then Ki went to the back door.

Immediately he saw that the old padlock that secured the door had been broken open. He pushed against the door and it gave way easily. Someone was inside, he was certain. The rusty door hinge groaned as he stepped in. He stopped to listen. In the front room he heard something: the sound of boots shuffling on the floor. And from beneath the door that separated Kelso's office from the outer room he saw wisps of gray smoke curling out.

Before he could make a move for the middle door, it burst open. Ki saw the outline of a man, and beyond he could see the flames licking up from the floor. At first the man did not notice Ki. He carried an unlit kerosene lamp. He stopped to light it. Ki stood stock-still to see what the man would do next.

When the lamp was lit, the man, who wore a floppy-brimmed hat that concealed his face, moved toward the desk. Ki said, "What are you doing here?"

Startled, the man dropped the lamp as he looked up. Then he dove quickly to his right, drawing a revolver as he fell. He triggered two rounds at the spot where Ki had been standing. But before the shots exploded in his ears, Ki too had jumped to one side. Without a gun, the Oriental was at a disadvantage in the enclosed space. He kept low as another blast ricocheted off the wall over his head.

Then, suddenly, the spilled kerosene, which had spread over the floor beneath the broken lamp, ignited. Ki heard the man curse. Another shot rang out as the man scrambled to his feet and bolted for the back door. As he ran, he picked up a chair and heaved it at Ki. The samurai rolled across the floor toward the exploding flame, and barely avoided the chair as it smashed into the wall. He leaped up and lunged for the fleeing man. But the arsonist was a step ahead of Ki and reached the door, swinging it open and running outside.

Ki had to choose whether to stay and fight the fire or to pursue the man. Already the back room was filling up with clouds of smoke, and from the front he could hear the crackle of the spreading flames. Realizing it was probably more than one man could handle, he turned his back on the fire and ran out the door.

As he hit the night air he ducked just in time to avoid a bullet that snapped past his ear. The man stood twenty feet away, at the mouth of the alley, and leveled his revolver for another shot at his pursuer. Ki reached into a pocket of his vest and felt for a *shuriken* throwing star. With the blade in his nimble fingers he whipped it out and, in one smooth, quick motion, sent it sailing at the arsonist.

The sharp, whirling star spun at the man's gun hand, slicing through a layer of flesh just as he squeezed the trigger. The shot went wild as the gun flew from his injured hand. He howled in pain and fright.

By this time Ki had selected another weapon, more accurate and penetrating at this greater range: a double-ended dart about six inches long. He watched as the man turned to run up the dark alleyway. With a lightning-fast flick of his wrist, Ki released the pencil-like weapon. This one caught the man's shirt right at the back of his neck, the sharp point pinning the cloth against the wall of the next-door building. As the firebug struggled to pull himself free, Ki ran at him. The man reached behind his neck to yank the shirt free, cutting his fingers on the other end of the razor-sharp dart. With both hands bloodied now, he cried out.

Ki was upon him before he knew it. With a swift, slicing chop of his open hand, the samurai closed the man's mouth and rocked his head back hard against the shingled wall. That shut him up and he slumped to the ground, his bleeding hands falling in the dust. Ki recovered the dart from the wall and replaced it in his pocket. He lifted the arsonist and carried him out of the alley and into the street, where he dumped him.

There, in the glowing light from the flames at the front of the building, he saw the man's face clearly for the first time. The arsonist was Darrel.

Rushing back into the Starbuck building, he found the fire climbing the walls. Tongues of yellow flame lashed at the wooden furniture and the papers and books. He could not make it to the front room because a sheet of fire barred the door. The heat and smoke were intense. Ki covered his face to protect it, and stumbled back out the door.

He found Darrel still lying in the street, unconscious. But by this time a crowd of townspeople had gathered at the scene. Someone shouted for water, and several men broke away to fetch buckets. The nearest source was a horse trough across the wide street. With much chattering and pointing, the people formed a line and waited for the buckets to arrive.

Ki bent over the arsonist and shook him by the shoulders. The man groaned and mumbled something incomprehensible. Ki shook him again. This time he got a response; Darrel opened his eyes slightly and started choking. Ki slapped his face and Darrel came fully awake. "Oh, God, my head!" he exclaimed. "What the hell happened?"

"How did you get out of jail?" Ki demanded.

"What—I—" Darrel suddenly realized what was happening. His head had fallen to the ground, revealing his ugly face and misshapen nose. His ears were big, his jaw long and unshaven. Ki guessed that he hadn't set the fire for fun—he wasn't smart enough for that, or to engineer a jailbreak. Someone had put him up to it.

The men finally returned with the buckets, and the line started to work. But it soon became apparent to them that their effort was too little, too late. Hot yellow tongues of fire darted from the windows of the building, sending heat and sparks into the street. The men of Gilead started throwing the water on the neighboring structures to prevent the fire from spreading. If they contained it, only the one building would be lost and there would be no danger to the rest of the town.

More onlookers gathered as smoke and flames rose into the night sky. They stood gawking and pointing, talking among themselves. Few took notice of Ki and the downed arsonist.

"Why did you do it?" Ki said. "Who paid you?"

Darrel shook his head and clamped his mouth shut. Fear scored his eyes as he looked into the angry samurai's face. He hadn't expected to be caught in the act. Something had gone terribly wrong. "I ain't sayin' nothin'," he mumbled.

Jessie arrived just then, running to the scene in her elegant green dress. She took it all in with a glance and saw Ki kneeling over the man, questioning him. "Ki!" she shouted. "Are you all right? What's happening?"

Ki said, without looking up, "This man set fire to the office. I arrived too late to stop him."

"Who is he?" Jessie asked, bending over the man pinned to the ground by Ki's strong hands on his shoulders. Then she saw it was Darrel.

Ki himself was breathing heavily, his black hair hanging down over his eyes, his face blackened from smoke and soot. He was angry, and would have broken the man's neck right there if she asked him to. She wondered how in God's name Darrel had gotten out of jail. That damned Lowell! Drunk on the job again.

"How did he get out?" she asked. "Why did he come back?"

Ki shook the man violently. Jessie was afraid he'd rattle the fellow's brains to mush before he could talk. "He won't tell you anything," she said.

"He doesn't wish to talk," her companion stated. "He doesn't know how unwise a choice that is. I'll make him talk if you want, Jessie. I'll make him hurt so bad he'll tell us everything."

Darrel gurgled in protest, his eyes wide with fear.

Jessie stood and watched the flames eat their way into the roof of the building. It was lost, along with all the records inside. *Damn them,* she cursed inwardly. Her only source of satisfaction was the thought of how she had left Winslow after their encounter just moments ago—and the letter she had seen.

"Let's take him back to the jailhouse," she said. "There's nothing more to do here."

"I didn't do nothin'," Darrel protested. He struggled to his feet, Ki supporting him. "It was—it was an accident."

"Save your lies for the sheriff," she told him. She smelled liquor on his breath. Whoever put him up to the crime had oiled him up with whiskey and sent him out to do his job. If she could get him to talk, she'd have solid evidence against her unseen enemy. And since she had just come from Winslow's suite, and had been with him for over an hour, it seemed unlikely that he had ordered the torching of the office. Or was it? Was he clever enough to stay one step removed from Darrel, assuring himself of a viable alibi by having Jessie over?

Ki held Darrel upright with his arms under the hapless arsonist's armpits. As they moved away from the fire and headed toward the jailhouse, a gunshot shattered the dark night.

Darrel didn't have time to scream. The bullet crashed into his forehead and exited out the back of his skull, carrying with it a spray of fragments of bone and blood and gray matter. Ki let the man drop like a limp rag onto the street, his ears picking up the location of the shooter: the top of a livery stable just across the street. Whoever it was had placed an excellent shot—and had silenced Darrel forever.

Darting through the bucket brigade, Ki streaked for the

livery. He arrived at the back of the building just in time to see a man riding away in the darkness. He hadn't had a chance to get a good look. Frustrated, he returned to Jessie.

She was bent over the dead man as a small knot of people gathered around to witness the gory sight. She looked up at Ki with tears in her eyes. He waved the townspeople away.

"Ki, what's happening here?"

"I don't know, Jessie." He helped her to her feet. "Let's return to your room. You must get some sleep if we are to ride tomorrow."

Back at the hotel, Ki stepped into the room before her. Establishing that there wasn't yet another bushwhacker present, he lighted her lamp. She sat on the bed, her evening dress wrinkled and soiled, her hair in disarray. She told Ki of her session with Winslow. He laughed when she explained how she had drugged him and got hold of the letter.

"And what did the letter say?"

"I don't quite know what to make of it," she said. "I copied it down." She handed the copy to Ki, who read it with a puzzled expression on his face.

Winslow—

Our arrangement is threatened by the Starbuck woman and her companion. If you do not deal with them, I shall be forced to. And if you fail, I shall deal with you accordingly. We travel to Beacon tomorrow to conclude business there. If, upon my return to Gilead, you have not fulfilled your commitment, you will live just long enough to regret it.

Sincerely,
J.G.

"Winslow knows about the Beacon project that Kelso was working on. How much, I'm not sure. He offered to

72

throw in with the Starbuck company, to put up money. I don't know what to make of it. And who's J.G.?"

"It looks like Winslow is serving another master, the man called J.G. We may run into him in Beacon, whoever he is."

"What does he want from us, Ki?"

"Get some sleep, Jessie. We must ride out early. Our questions will be answered in Beacon—or they'll not be answered at all. We'll leave Winslow behind to stew in his own juices, as your father used to say."

"Something inside makes me want to feel sorry for Winslow. Could be he's playing for higher stakes than he planned. Whatever his game is."

Steel Knife explained to Julius Goodpaster how he had silenced Darrel Kinchloe. The carnival master swirled his brandy in a balloon glass. A lone lamp cast an eerie glow throughout the wagon's interior. It was late; it had been a busy day, but there remained much to be done.

"And you delivered the letter to Winslow?"

"Yes," the half-breed said.

"That'll give him something to chew on, the bastard. I don't trust him. He's too ambitious and not smart enough to see beyond his own greedy interests. We could have made a mistake with Winslow, but we must make do. Too late now to approach any of the other businessmen in Gilead. I'm thinking that Mohart might have been a better bet. He's cold-blooded and not quite as pompous as our hotel baron." Goodpaster laughed quietly to himself and took a generous swallow of the fine dark brandy.

Steel Knife watched him. He kept his mouth shut unless spoken to. He waited for Goodpaster's final orders.

"We leave in the morning for Beacon. Make sure the wagons are secured and the teams ready. And watch Heany—the son of a bitch is liable to drink himself silly if we don't keep an eye on him. He's got to be in shape to whip that boy in Beacon, if it's the last time he fights." Goodpaster considered the rich brown liquor in his glass. "And it very well may be. He's all washed up. Good night, Steel Knife."

The half-breed exited into the night without a word, leaving Goodpaster to enjoy his fine brandy.

It occurred to the carnival owner then that he'd better assign two or three men to keep an eye on Miss Starbuck and the Oriental, to watch their movements and prevent them from further interference with his plans. If necessary, he'd arrange for the strange pair to turn up dead. He smiled at the thought.

Chapter 5

At sunup, Jessie and Ki rode out for Beacon. Jessie sat her
saddle atop a tall sorrel mare with good spirit and strength.
Ki rode a spotted gray gelding with a black mane and tail.
Carrying enough provisions for the day's ride, they set an
even pace. Ki was in a quiet mood, thinking about the girl
Yvonne, and the events of the past few days. Jessie, too,
did not say much; she was preoccupied with Winslow's
double dealings and this man J.G., a cipher to her still.

The riders were a striking pair. Jessie wore her tight
denim pants, tall black boots with small-roweled Texas spurs,
her blue cambric blouse open at the neck, and a snug leather
vest hugging her breasts. Atop her head, the flat-crowned
hat did little to cover the mass of reddish-gold hair that
streamed out from beneath it. Ki was garbed as usual in his
leather vest, black and many-pocketed. He too had on blue
denim trousers, and his customary rope-soled slippers, and

from his waistband protruded the *tanto* knife. He carried his *katana* long sword, war bow, and lacquered *ebira* quiver on his saddle, within easy reach. Jessie's converted .38-caliber Colt revolver rode in its holster on her belt, and she kept a new Winchester .44-40 rifle in a saddle boot behind her leg.

As the sun rose over them in the clear, sea-blue sky, they filled their lungs with the clean air of the Nebraska plains. Although the country was mostly flat, it was broken occasionally by low-lying hills and slow-running creeks. They passed a farmhouse now and then, but did not see any people for the entire morning.

"The Oglala Sioux used to roam here," said Jessie at one point, as they crested a knoll and could see the surrounding country for miles. "I wonder if these farmers are making better use of the land than the Indians did."

Ki said, "I've known few white people who cared as much for their land as the Indians do—or did. Who can say whether it is better to break the land and plant crops or to live with the land and hunt on it? But the Indians' time is past," he concluded. "The white man has made sure of that."

"Their spirit is still here," Jessie said, almost reverently. Within her she felt a strange feeling welling up, a mixture of awe and grief. She could not change history, but she could not help wondering how things might have been if the white man had learned to exist with the red man, instead of driving him off his ancestral lands. The basin that stretched out before them was a fertile, beautiful chunk of God's earth. And the white man had to possess it all for himself; that was the way he worked and there was no changing it.

Around noon, with six hours of riding behind them, they stopped to rest and water the horses in the shade of an ash copse by a narrow stream. A few high clouds dotted the bright sky, and the day promised to get hotter. Jessie and Ki drank water and chewed on some jerked beef. The meat was rugged-tasting, but it put something in their stomachs. They had corked their canteens and started back to their mounts when the first shot rang out.

A bullet whipped by Jessie's face and buried itself in a tree. Instantly, Ki pushed her to the ground behind a fallen tree trunk. Two more shots sliced the air and their animals whinnied in fright.

Ki snaked back toward his horse and took his bow and quiver from the saddle. He tossed the weapons to the ground and went for Jessie's Winchester. Hot lead peppered the leaves overhead. He unsheathed her rifle, scooped up his own weapons, and rejoined Jessie behind the log.

"Can you see them?" she asked.

Ki peered out in the direction of the booming guns. He saw powdersmoke, but he could not see their attackers. The two horses crossed the stream and galloped off. They'd have to round up the animals later, when the shooting stopped. But first they must face these infernal bushwhackers, whoever they were.

"No, I cannot see them," Ki replied. He crawled forward several feet on his belly, dragging the bow and the quiver full of war arrows. Pulling himself up against a tree for cover, he quickly strung the bow and tested it. He then nocked an arrow on the gut string and waited.

Jessie, meanwhile, moved up beside him, then took cover behind a nearby tree. The attack commenced again, bullets spanging off the trees and digging into the soft ground. Ki watched intently, trying to gauge the exact source of the attack. He pinpointed it on the side of a hill about thirty yards distant. And listening to the sound of the gunfire, he came to another conclusion. "There are three of them, Jessie. One on the south side of the hill, two to the north. See the smoke from their guns."

Jessie looked where he directed her, and she could see that he was right. Another volley came their way. In the stillness of the open plain, the gunshots crashed and echoed.

Though they were shaded by the ash trees, the heat was becoming more intense. Combined with the acrid smell of burnt powder, it made for a feeling of closeness, of entrapment.

Ki raised his bow, supporting himself on one knee, and let a steel-tipped war arrow fly. It sailed in a gentle but swift arc over the breast of the hill. The samurai heard a shout. The men ceased firing for a minute. When the shooting began again, there were only two gunmen at work.

With her Winchester, Jessie sent several rounds in the direction of the man on the south side of the knoll. Her bullets were ineffective. She felt the rifle barrel becoming hot as she fired round after round in rapid succession. Sweat rolled down her temples as she tried to concentrate on her distant target. She squeezed the trigger once again, and the long-barreled rifle roared. Dirt kicked up at the attacker's head and he was silent for a while—probably reloading, she thought.

Her companion sent two more arrows flying at the hillside. But the attackers kept firing. Lead flew into the small woods. Jessie judged that the bushwhackers couldn't be too bright if they had attacked her and Ki in this situation, rather than waiting until they were back on the open trail. But now that the move had been made, she was determined to make them pay for it—and to find out who the hell they were. She had a good idea already.

"Let's move up to the treeline," Ki suggested. "Stay low and keep the trees between you and them."

Jessie loosed another shot before she and Ki edged forward. Crawling on her belly and elbows, Jessie cursed to herself. Although she always fought, and fought hard, when forced to do so, she did not like eating dirt any more than anyone else. She saw herself riding into Beacon—if they made it that far—as dirty as a cowhand after two months on the trail. But she put all such thoughts behind her as she reached her new position and raised her rifle again.

Ki waited out the attackers, drawing a more careful bead on the gunsmoke of the one to his right. With an arrow on the bow and the string drawn taut, he took slow, careful aim. This time he did not give his shot such a high arc. Allowing for the steady pull of gravity and the distance the arrow must travel, he released an almost straight-line shot. The arrow sped forward. Ki saw the tip of the man's hat disappear as the shaft snatched it away. But apparently the bushwhacker was not hurt, because he renewed his fire even more savagely.

It looked as if his first arrow had used up all the luck he was allowed for one day. It had taken one man out, but he was having no further success. He'd have to change position once again, to give himself a better angle to work from.

"Jessie," he called out as she was reloading her Winchester. "Cover me. I'm going to move to that rock over there." He pointed to a rock that jutted from the ground about ten yards north of the copse. It was not a large one, and there was a lot of open ground between it and the trees.

"Be careful, Ki," she said. But she knew she could not dissuade him once his mind was made up. As he got to his feet and began to run, crouching low, she opened fire. Through the smoke of her own rifle, she chambered six rounds one after another and scattered them at both sides of the small hill. It was enough to keep the attackers silent as Ki darted to the rock.

Once there, the samurai was kept inactive by a heavy dose of lead from the bushwhackers. But they couldn't ignore Jessie for long, and soon they were dividing their attention between the two. This was just what Ki had counted on. He selected a carefully crafted and balanced war arrow from the sturdy *ebira* quiver. He checked the tip, a broad steel blade that was wide enough to sever a man's head if shot from close range. The rifle fire continued all about him, but he lay quietly, patiently, awaiting his opportunity.

Jessie kept up her heavy barrage, but did not feel the

tide turning. She wondered how seriously the first man was injured, the one Ki had caught with an arrow. And there were still two able-bodied men throwing lead at them. She pumped furiously, orange flame spitting from the barrel mouth of her gun. The attackers answered her, shot for shot. Then, when she was down to two rounds, there was a brief silence. The men must be reloading again

For Ki, this was the break he had waited for. He rose to one knee, steadying himself with the other leg outthrust. He drew back the powerful bow, leveled his aim, and sent the big-tipped arrow streaking toward his target. He had calculated where the man's collarbone must be, and hoped he'd be in the vicinity.

A loud cry erupted from behind the hill. Ki's arrow had found flesh. Again, though, it was impossible to know how much damage it had caused.

The remaining gunman kept firing, and bullets chewed up the ground near Jessie's position. Determined to do some damage herself, she patiently prepared for her best opportunity, holding her Winchester snugly to her shoulder and steadying the gunsights on the distant target—what there was of it. The bushwhacker, who had now seen his two comrades take Ki's arrows, fired rapidly, almost desperately, scattering lead from Jessie's position to where Ki hugged the meager cover the jutting rock afforded him. His bare head popped into the open with each shot at Ki.

Squinting in the shimmering sun-haze, Jessie calmly squeezed off a shot when the man held his head up just a split second too long. The rifle roared in her ears. The bullet sliced off the top of the attacker's scalp and sent him hurtling back, his skull open and blood spilling out of the gaping wound.

Quickly but cautiously, Jessie and Ki forsook their cover and advanced on the hill. Jessie had at least ten rounds left in her weapon, and Ki held an arrow at the ready. Cresting the hill, they looked down on the hapless bushwhackers, two dead and one severely injured.

Ki warily checked the dead ones. The man with part of his head missing was already making a feast for the flies. The other, with Ki's wide-tipped war arrow in his breast, lay in grotesque protest, stiffening beneath the open blue sky. The samurai turned away in disgust.

Jessie bent over the wounded man, who had taken Ki's first arrow in the neck. It had just missed severing the artery and was tilted down at a dangerous angle toward his spinal cord. The bushwhacker had gone white and was groaning like a sick bull. She did not touch him for fear of bringing on a fresh flow of blood that he could ill afford to lose. He opened his eyes and saw her and tried to spit, but only succeeded in drooling obscenely.

"Who are you?" she asked.

The man rasped, "I ain't talkin'. Not...gonna say nothin'..."

Ki came and stood over the downed man. "Tell her what she wants to know," he commanded.

"What're you—a goddamned yeller Injun, with them arrows? Go ahead and kill me, 'cause—" he gasped for breath and wrinkled his face in pain—"'cause I ain't talkin'.'"

"Just tell me who hired you," said Jessie. "Why did they want us dead? Was it Winslow?"

"No fuckin' way," the hardcase croaked. Dressed in dirty trail clothes like his dead companions, he looked the part of an accomplished backshooter—a perfect man for the job, until he had run into Jessie and Ki.

"Kill me...kill me," he begged suddenly. "I won't squeal."

Jessie looked at Ki in exasperation. The man moved, trying to raise himself on his elbows. He still had considerable strength left, though he knew he was a dead man.

Ki took hold of the feathered end of the shaft. The bushwhacker's eyes windened in fear. Ki twisted the arrow slightly and the man screamed loud enough to rouse the spirits of the dead tribes. "Oh, Jesus! Don't do that!" he bellowed. "Kill me! Kill me!"

"Not until you tell us what we want," Ki said tonelessly, hating to torture the man, but having no other choice.

"Goddamn..." Tears welled in the sunken sockets and rolled down his ashen face. "Help me sit up. I'll talk."

Ki eased the man up, resting his back against a tree. The arrow hung suspended, both ends sticking out of his neck. A trickle of blood ran across his throat. He choked on the words: "It was Goodpaster...Julius Goodpaster. Runs the carnival show. Don't...know why. Paid us twenty dollars...each." He labored for air and sweated from the effort of fighting the pain.

"Goodpaster?" Jessie looked puzzled. "Our mystery man, J.G. You hear of him, Ki?"

"No. The carnival is in Gilead."

The gunman rocked his head back and forth. "They ...moved out...this morning. Oh, Jesus!" He gave out a bloodcurdling shriek.

"What else do you know?" Jessie asked through gritted teeth. She had seen death before—lots of it. But this man's suffering was almost too much to bear. "Didn't he say anything else?"

"Not a goddamn—nothing." The words spilled out in spurts as he gulped to get oxygen to his lungs. "I wouldn't tell you..."

"You've already told us what we want to know," she said. Then she looked at Ki and nodded. She stood and walked away, unable to watch.

Ki placed his bow and arrow on the ground and unsheathed his *ko-dachi* knife. With one swift, clean stoke he sliced the attacker's throat open and released him from this life.

• • •

Beacon lay scattered on the plain, a seemingly random jumble of ramshackle frame buildings that looked as though they had never been painted. It reminded Jessie of an old buffalo hunters' trading post she'd seen once on the Staked Plains in West Texas—jerry-built and temporary and unappealing. But people still lived in Beacon and were keeping it alive, if barely.

They had buried the three men in hastily dug graves back at the site of the ambush. Now, as the sun set in flaming splendor over the stark, beautiful plain, they had reached their destination—tired, frustrated, angry, and even more confused by this new twist in their pursuit of the truth behind Kelso's death.

"Who the hell is Julius Goodpaster, and why is he throwing twenty dollars at bushwhackers?" Jessie muttered aloud, the question that had been plaguing her all afternoon. "What are we to him?"

"I'll wire Omaha, the U.S. marshal's office," said Ki. "They might know."

"Good idea." It was the only idea they were likely to come up with. Jessie traced back over the events of the past three days, trying to tie this latest episode in. Somehow it didn't fit. What did the traveling carnival show have to do with this whole mess? She asked Ki what he knew about the show. Ki told her what he and Yvonne had seen, but had no knowledge of Goodpaster. He too wondered how this new man figured in.

"Send it first thing," Jessie added. "I have a feeling we don't have much time."

But it wasn't long before they discovered just how close their new enemy was. As they rode into town they saw posters nailed to every post and doorway, fluttering in the slight breeze. Ki dismounted and snatched one down, taking it back to Jessie. What they read turned their blood cold.

The bill advertised a bizarre challenge to the community of Beacon, which, according to the last paragraph, the town had accepted. In short, the American Carnival Entertainment Company had put up ten thousand dollars against the entire town of Beacon—lock, stock, and barrel—in a wager to be decided by a boxing match pitting the carnival's champion, Dennis Heany, against a representative of the town. Winner take all. "The above described agreement having been endorsed in writing, by the citizens of Beacon, Nebraska, the match shall take place two days hence at twelve o'clock noon in the town square. All and sundry are invited to attend." And the document was signed "J. Goodpaster, Proprietor."

"What do you make of this?" Jessie asked Ki. "I can't believe an entire town would agree to this farce."

In the street, groups of men gathered, talking and waving their arms. They took due notice of the two strange riders, but made no overtures toward Jessie and Ki. Soon they were all gathered together in a crowd that numbered more than twenty, some of them shouting, others standing on the fringes with resignation on their faces.

"I've never seen such a queer sight," said Jessie. "What's happening here?"

"White men are the strangest race I've ever encountered," Ki replied. "I have ceased to be surprised by them."

"But the whole town—they're betting their town on some fight that's got to be rigged. And if they lose—Goodpaster owns the whole thing." It struck her then. Of course! Whoever owned Beacon most surely owned the rights to petroleum and whatever other minerals lay beneath it. She turned to Ki. "Take care of the horses. And go right to the telegraph office and send that wire to Omaha. The more I hear of this Goodpaster fellow, the less I like him."

Jessie dismounted. She meant to take a look around, find the man who had been working with Kelso, get some answers. Hovering behind the crowd, she looked across the street.

The young man stood apart from the other townspeople, his powerful arms crossed over his chest and a wry half-smile playing on his lips. He was well over six feet tall, with broad shoulders and a tapering torso, long legs, and an erect posture. His rough but handsome features were crowned by a mass of dark, wavy hair, and his eyes were a warm brown. He looked very much like a blacksmith.

When the crowd began to disperse, Jessie walked over to him. He met her look frankly, sizing her up without being too obvious about it, the way most men were when confronted with her beauty. "My name is Dale Knowlton," he said.

"Jessie Starbuck." They shook hands and she felt the strength and confidence of his firm grip. "You're the man I've been looking for."

"I'm not surprised," he said diffidently. "I heard they killed Kelso. I figured something was going on."

She noticed he was not wearing a weapon. This was unusual for a man in a town like Beacon, where the only law was gun law. But somehow Knowlton gave off an aura of strength that seemed protection enough against any sort of threat. She liked that about him. And she liked the dancing gleam in his soft brown eyes. She wanted to know more about him.

"What do you think of this insane challenge by Goodpaster?" Jessie asked him.

"Not so insane. He knows what he's doing. But he's going to lose."

"Why do you say that?"

"Because I'm the ox who's going to fight his man in the ring."

"You're joking," she said. "I hear that Heany is a monster. What's more, they won't let you win."

"If I step into the ring, I'll win," Knowlton stated. It

was no brag; it was as if he were assuring her that the sun would rise tomorrow.

Jessie shook her head, her golden-red locks swaying brightly. "It's not that I doubt you, Dale. But I don't trust Goodpaster. Some of his men attacked me on my way here. My friend Ki and I had to kill them. He won't allow anyone to win this crazy bet with the town. He has too much at stake."

"So do I," Knowlton said. "I wouldn't accept the challenge if I didn't think I could win."

Jessie changed the subject, explaining why she and Ki had come to Beacon, and she told Knowlton all she knew about Kelso's death. "What did Kelso tell you?" she wanted to know.

"Nothing, really. I went along with him on his explorations, helped him set up his surveying equipment. I drove the wagon, but he never said much to me. I agreed to assemble the drill he was going to order. I'm a blacksmith by trade."

"Most blacksmiths I know are always busy," she said with a smile.

"Beacon is bad for business—of any kind," he replied. "Folks are moving out faster than they're coming in. I make a few wheel rims, shoe a few horses. Not enough to keep me busy for more than two or three hours a day. That's why I was so interested in Kelso's doings. There was a chance to make some good money for a change."

"He did talk about money, then," Jessie gently prodded.

"He said there could be a lot of money in his discovery, if it was handled right. Promised me a cut if I stuck with him."

"I don't believe that you haven't figured it out by now, even if he didn't tell you what it was."

Knowlton couldn't help smiling at this pretty, smart-as-a-whip lady. A Starbuck from Texas. Probably rode like a Comanche and danced like a fancy English lady—quite a combination. His instinct was to be blunt with her, to hold back nothing. He said, "Oil, I figure. But there's not a hell of a lot of money in that, is there?"

"If the deposit is large enough. if it can produce ten or twenty barrels a day. There's talk of running steam engines with oil rather than coal. Back in Ohio, this Mr. Rockefeller started organizing companies about ten years ago to drill for it and refine it. And there's a lot of talk about it down in the Indian Territory. I don't know if anything will come of it, but folks are trying real hard to figure out how to use the stuff for more things than just lamp oil."

The tall young man nodded. "Kelso was always one to look ahead, to try new things. He was always reading up on things."

"Before his office was destroyed, I found several books and stacks of notes he had written. But I didn't get a chance to save them. All I've got is this map, and a copy of his letter to you."

As she produced the map to show him, Knowlton said, "Who was it torched his place? Not that I'm surprised."

"A fellow named Darrel Kinchloe, who somehow got out of jail after he attacked us at the office the night before. Sheriff's not telling how he got out, but I suspect this man Goodpaster had something to do with it. You knew Kelso had enemies?"

"Sure, I suspicioned it. When I heard he was dead, I knew somebody did it on purpose—to keep him quiet for good. No matter what the damned sheriff said. Somebody was threatened by his scheme, or wanted a piece of it."

"Who could have known of it? If you say he never confided in you, why would he tell anyone else about it?"

"I don't know. But they found out. Whoever they were."

"Well, what do you think of the map?"

"Familiar territory. Me and Kelso covered every inch. I'll take you out there if you like."

"Yes, I'd like that very much. The sooner the better.

Before this fight business. You sure you want to fight, Dale?"

"I said I don't mean to lose. These Beacon folks are fools, but I won't let them down."

"But what if you do lose? The town will be dead. How will you survive?" As she spoke with Knowlton, Jessie became more acutely aware of his quiet, unobtrusive strength. He was muscular, all right, but not ostentatiously so. He wore a loose-fitting linen shirt that did not cling to his powerful upper body. A smile played on his lips.

"I guess I didn't make myself clear. I said I don't plan to lose. I'm not boasting, but I know I can beat that Heany."

"You must be the only person who thinks so. From the long faces in town, it looks like they all expect to lose."

"That's why they will lose, eventually," he said bitterly. "They don't know what they want, and they're not willing to fight for it. They gave up a long time ago. If only they could see what we have in Beacon; it's not much, but it's a start. Hell, this could be a damn fine town. A place to have kids and bring them up right. Land all around to farm, maybe to raise some cows. I've been in a lot worse places."

"Like where?" Jessie found herself asking, interested in finding out more about this handsome young man. He was so tall that she barely came up to his shoulders.

"I was in the army for near ten years. Saw some action down in the Arizona Territory, chasing the Apache. Never knew thirst until I set foot in that godforsaken land. Got wounded once, nothing serious. Learned the soldiering trade from a big old colored fellow name of Joshua Johnson. He was a good man. Saw him killed—in a fight with a drunken sergeant. Wasn't a fair fight. Johnson would've won if it was. The sergeant pulled a knife and gutted old Joshua. Never brought to trial for it, neither. You know who that sergeant was, Miss Starbuck?"

Jessie shook her head, touched by the blacksmith's sad tale.

"The drunken sergeant was Dennis Heany, and I mean to kill him day after tomorrow."

"Does anybody else in town know about this?" Jessie asked him.

"No," said Knowlton. "And I figure you're not going to tell them."

"Of course not," she said. "But why did you tell me?"

"I wanted to tell somebody. It seems all right to tell you."

"Does Heany know who you are?"

"He'll find out soon enough—before he dies."

Knowlton turned and walked away. The gathering night cast the town in a dark shroud. Jessie hesitated, then followed him. There was something about him—his strength and reserve coupled with his boyish uncertainty—that made her want to stay with him. And she felt that under it all was an anger, a seething rage, ready to explode when touched off. If anyone could save the town, it was this big, quiet man with the powerful arms and short-fuse temper.

He had taken a dozen steps before he realized she was behind him. He stopped and waited for her to catch up.

Jessie and Knowlton walked side by side to the edge of town. The silence between them was not a barrier but a coming together. They were reaching out to each other. A half moon illuminated their path as they reached the edge of town.

The burly young man said, "I know a spot where we can sit and talk."

"I'd like that," said Jessie.

They crossed a narrow, cold stream that bubbled on its way, then they climbed a small hill. On the other side of the hill was a wood of tall conifers and poplar trees. In the gentle nighttime breeze, the treetops waved majestically and the poplar leaves whispered to them. Dale found a place where the trees opened to admit the sky. It reminded Jessie of a cathedral she had seen once: tall, dark, domed, a beautiful and mysterious vault that opened up to the heavens. They sat on the soft, cool bed of fallen needles and leaves.

"I come out here all the time," Knowlton said. "To be alone. To do my thinking."

"What do you think about?" she asked.

"Oh, about everything. About what I'm doing here, where I'm going, where I've come from. You probably can't imagine what a fellow like me could have to think about all the time. But I've got plenty on my mind."

"Of course you do. Don't say that about me. I could tell when we first met that you're carrying a lot around inside you. Do you want to tell me about it?"

She hoped he would. Inside this gentlemanly giant, something was waiting to explode. She could see it in his eyes, hear it in his even voice. He was carrying around a lot of hurt that was warring with his natural instinct to do good. In a violent town like Beacon, there must have been a lot of times when he was tried to the point of breaking, but apparently he never had broken. So far, he had bottled it all inside. Time was running out, though, and he was waiting now for the fight with Heany. Then he'd let it all loose, the devil take the hindmost. She only hoped that he'd prove equal to the match with the professional fighter that Ki had told her about. There was no doubt that Dale Knowlton was an immensely strong and agile man; but a wily ring veteran might have some tricks up his sleeve ready to pull on an inexperienced challenger.

He sat there with his knees drawn up to his chin. He looked at her. "There's a lot I'd like to tell you, Jessie. A whole lot."

"Look, Dale, I'm here to help—to do whatever I can for Beacon and for you. That oil land, if that's what it is, won't go to Goodpaster or Winslow or any of them. My partner, Ki, is here too. You can trust us. We've got so little to go on. Anything else you know—"

The blacksmith said, "I've told you as much as I know.

And damn, it isn't worth a hill of beans. I should have been more alert when Kelso asked me to work with him. If there was some other clue—if I had known he was in danger. I just never figured he'd end up dead. If I'd of known that . . . hell, I don't know what I could've done."

"You'd do the right thing, whatever it was," she reassured him

"The only right thing is to kill the man who killed Kelso. But I've got my mind on killing one man for now. I can't rest until I've done that. And I aim to do it fair and square—with my bare fists. No hidden knives this time. Then I can look for Kelso's killer. He can expect the same treatment."

"There's no call for that, Dale. There's already been too much killing. You concentrate on the fight. I don't want to see you hurt."

Knowlton smiled. "You're the first one's ever said that to me, Jessie. I've never had anybody to care about me, since I was a boy. Both my ma and pa were put under by smallpox down in East Texas. I was brought up by an aunt in Topeka, Kansas. Ran away from her and her do-good church soon as I could—when I was sixteen. Drifted right away into the army. That was all I knew for a long time. It was only when I set up business here in Beacon that I started to feel like I'd accomplish something. And I started yearning for a woman to share it with, too."

"Why, there are probably a dozen girls in Beacon who'd give their right arms—"

"Last time I counted, there were exactly five unmarried women in town. One is an old spinster, the second is fourteen, with freckles, and the other three work in a house over on the south end of town. I know one of them, Elizabeth, but she's not the marrying kind."

Jessie had to laugh. "If you lived in Austin or El Paso, you'd have so many to choose from it'd make your head spin."

"Well, I'll maybe just move down there and see for

91

myself," Knowlton said. "When this is all over with."

"You'd leave Beacon even after you've won?"

"Hell, this town is dead, Jessie. I told you. They're all worn out here, tired of trying. I don't know, though. If there was something to keep me here..."

"I just hate to see you take a chance on getting hurt if it's all for nothing."

"It's not for nothing. I keep remembering old Johnson. He's worth fighting for, even if these other bastards aren't."

Jessie knelt beside him. She smoothed back his hair. She wanted so much to comfort him, to help him, to feel the strength in his arms. It had been a long time since she'd felt attracted to a man so quickly. Yet there was a special essence to Dale Knowlton, an aura of power and quiet intelligence. It brought out a secret longing in her.

"Ten days ago," she said, "I'd never heard of Beacon or Goodpaster or Winslow or Heany. And I'd never heard of you. Suddenly, though, all of you are very important to me—especially you, Dale. I can't bear the thought of you matching fists with Heany, for whatever reason."

Dale put an arm around her slender shoulders, his hand brushing her soft golden hair. His large hand cupped her arm and he pulled her to him. "Hell, Jessie, I feel safe as a baby right now. We got a little time together, you and me."

"We sure do," she replied, dropping her head onto his massive chest. She felt his breathing become heavier as she hugged him. Then she lifted her face to his and their lips met in a crushing kiss. He pressed hard, trying to devour her, and she responded hungrily. She felt alive in his bear-like embrace.

Jessie looked up directly into Knowlton's eyes. She saw desire there that matched her own. She knew she could trust this big man. Most often, the men she met in her travels were more like Winslow—they wanted her to submit to them in one way or another. Jessie Starbuck, though, submitted to no man unless she felt she could trust him.

She had often thought about this matter of men and women; knowing that she had a body men desired, she nonetheless did not use it to advance herself or to gain anything. To her, the idea of using sex for gain was immoral; it was not immoral to lie with a man if she felt deep affection for him. Now, in the arms of the ruggedly handsome blacksmith, she did not have second thoughts. This time was theirs, and perhaps it would never come again.

Dale bent and kissed her, a warm, glancing touch of his lips upon hers. Jessie clasped her hands around his neck and pressed him closer, holding the kiss. He relaxed and enjoyed it. Their tongues meshed wetly, passionately.

After a few long minutes, Jessie pulled herself free of his embrace. She caught her breath and said, "Dale, I want to take your mind off Heany. For a while, at least. Come here, sit beside me." Jessie sat on the cool, grassy earth beneath the dark trees. Knowlton eased himself down at her side. She stroked his hair. "Please forget the fight. You'll do what you have to do. But for now, be with me."

"Jessie—I want you to know I've never been with any woman other than the bought kind, like Elizabeth."

Jessie laughed. "There's only one kind of woman. I'm sure the girls you've been with were glad to have you."

"Oh, I never treat 'em bad. It just isn't my way to do that. But I can't say as I've ever been in love, either. 'Cept as a kid once. I had a hankering for a preacher's daughter in Topeka."

"What was she like?" Jessie asked.

"Real pretty, with lots of blond curls and blue eyes. And she was a couple years older than me, already on her way to becoming a woman. She never knew I was around, I suppose. But that didn't keep me from dreaming about her. Never hurts to dream."

"No, I don't suppose it does." Jessie put her hand on his muscular arm. "I hope you haven't given up your dreams."

"No. Like I told you, I plan to do all right for myself one of these days. All I want is a decent-size spread and some beef—and a good woman for a wife. Then I can retire for good from the blacksmith business."

Her heart went out to him, this man of simple convictions and simple needs. She felt him shift his weight and move closer. His face met Jessie's for another kiss. This time he took the lead, probing her open mouth with his strong tongue. With his arms firmly around her shoulders, he lowered her to the ground, his mouth lingering on hers.

Jessie felt her breasts being crushed to her chest as he brought himself down atop her. She dug her fingers into his back and pulled him closer, the need rising within her.

"Jesus, Jessie," he whispered raggedly, "I want you so bad, gal."

"Take me, Dale. I want you to take me and love me."

He eased up a bit so as to be able to unbutton her shirt. He pulled it open to reveal her creamy white breasts. Touching them, grazing his work-roughened fingers over the round pink nipples, he wondered at their symmetry and beauty and softness. Jessie gasped as his hands and the frigid night breeze combined to bring her nipples erect; the slightest touch on their sensitive surface made her tingle inside. The blacksmith began to kiss her breasts, licking at the tender nipples, then he bit one lightly and sucked at it.

"God!" she cried. "That feels so nice, Dale." She ran her hands down his spine.

Dale devoured her, making her writhe beneath him. Finally he came up for air and found her lips plastered to his. Jessie fumbled to release him from his own shirt. When she had undone the buttons, he slipped free of it. His broad, hairy chest was the target for her fingers. She raked her nails across it, marveling at the strength and largeness of this man, wondering if all of him was this big....

By this time, Knowlton had her belt unbuckled. Jessie kicked off her boots and lifted her hips so that he could slip her pants off. He laid the pants on the ground beneath her and she relaxed, lying back, naked, in anticipation. Knowlton kissed her and ran his tongue down over her chin and neck, over her breasts to her stomach. She stifled a long moan. With his left hand he parted her legs and touched the soft flesh of her inner thighs. He ran his hand slowly up until he reached the softly thatched place where her legs met. He felt the heat and wetness there.

Jessie held his shoulders, her eyes tightly closed. Dale slowly rubbed a finger over the moist, tender skin of her sex. It made her shiver as he touched the slick folds and got closer to the core of excitement. Then his thick finger entered her. Her lips formed an oval of exquisite pleasure, but no sound came out. She reached out for his wrist and held his hand there. Knowlton flicked his thumb over the growing nub of flesh as he kept the finger buried inside her. Jessie sighed and clenched her teeth. She could no longer contain herself.

"Please, Dale, keep doing that! Oh, I want you to—oh!"

He kissed her again and again as he moved his finger in her. She opened and closed her legs around his hand, gulping in the night air with heaving lungs. "Please...please..." she whispered. He increased his tempo and she felt the wave of climax building inside her. Jessie relaxed and let him do the rest. His strong manipulations brought her closer and closer, until she began to feel the wave break over her.

Suddenly she came in a flood, whimpering in his ear, "Yes, yes, that feels good, Dale." She couldn't stop, and didn't want to. "Oh, oh—" Her words were choked off with his deep strokes. Then she went limp with a great sigh.

Knowlton withdrew his finger, now wet with her juices. As she lay there quietly, he removed his boots and pants and underwear. His erection jutted out in front of him like an ax handle. As he snuggled up against her, his manhood brushed her leg.

Jessie groped for it and, finding it, wrapped her hand

around its hard length. "Is this all yours?" she queried mischievously.

The blacksmith, struggling to speak as she squeezed him, managed to mutter, "Yeah, it's me."

"You should have warned me," she teased. She ran her fingers up and down the shaft, reaching down to heft the heavy sack that hung beneath it.

"The hell you say..." But now it was his turn to be stimulated into silence. He felt the growing tension as she massaged him slowly and with great care. In her hands his sex felt as stiff and strong as a redwood.

Unlike many women, Jessie was not afraid of sex; she enjoyed it and valued it for the pleasure it brought her— and her partner. With a man like Dale Knowlton, she knew the full flower of desire, smelling its fragrance, touching its soft petals. She was not shy about it, not now after having been brought to such a shattering orgasm. No, she did not want to withdraw now; she wanted to share with him the complete fulfillment he needed.

"Lie back," she told him. He did, and Jessie slid down beside him. She bathed the insides of his legs with her tongue, gently teasing him and running her hand up and down the backside of his thighs. He crouched down a bit more, his head resting against a tree. With one hand she stroked his manhood as she ran her tongue over it. She took her time, slowly working his erect organ with fingers and tongue, bringing him to painful attention. Then, suddenly, her whole mouth was around it.

Slowly at first, Jessie took nearly his entire length into her mouth, her darting tongue swirling around the shaft. He gripped her head with both hands and softly massaged her.

More rapidly, then, she sucked him. Knowlton felt the pressure building deep inside him, coursing from his brain to his stomach to his groin, a tension ready to explode at the back of his head as this beautiful young woman made tender yet painful love to him. She must have felt it too, for she stopped and squeezed the base of his manhood between her fingers.

"Jesus, Jessie," he exclaimed. "You've got to stop that."

She brought herself up alongside him and kissed him. Without a word, Knowlton shifted himself over on top of her as she opened her legs for him. Their naked bodies glistened with a thin patina of perspiration as they came together, the blacksmith entering her, seeking the source of the heat and the love that had compelled them toward this moment.

"Oh, darling, fill me up," Jessie cooed. She put her hands on his cool buttocks, pressing him for more.

Knowlton withdrew and plunged in with renewed force, then began to stroke rapidly. Her undulating body trembled as he drove harder and she took everything he gave, emitting little love cries into the night sky. He almost came right then, but held it back.

Jessie felt the wave breaking over her again.

"Christ, Jessie," Knowlton gasped. "I can't stop."

"Don't, don't, don't. Stay inside me. I want all of you."

They were writhing together in a mad, beautiful frenzy now, Knowlton's long, muscular body moving against hers, his sword plunging faster and faster into her sheath. She closed her eyes and gripped him, then splayed her legs wider. Knowlton held on; he fought release, but it was a losing battle. Jessie cried out in delight as she came, and he felt her muscles quivering around his bold weapon. Waves of pleasure rocked her as she was pinned beneath him.

Then he could hold out no longer. In a painful spasm of fulfillment, he exploded into her, causing Jessie to climax yet again. It was as if he were spilling the last drop of his life's juice. But if he had to die, he could choose no better way than in this woman's arms.

★

Chapter 6

After leaving Jessie, Ki saw to their horses and went to the telegraph office, where he wired the Omaha office of the U.S. marshal. He paid the operator a dollar to stay there and wait for a reply. The sooner he and Jessie knew more about Julius Goodpaster, the better.

He then went out to scout the town under the pretext of buying provisions. He attracted more than a few curious stares, as he inevitably did in a strange town. Lithe and erect, he crossed the main street and entered a general store. Several men were inside, two of them playing checkers and the others kibitzing idly—and talking about the big wager, no doubt. The shopkeeper, a stout man in his late fifties with thinning gray hair atop a red face, approached Ki.

"Can I help you, mister?" he asked.

"I need a few things," said Ki, sizing the man up quickly. He seemed friendly enough—like most good shopkeepers who wanted to attract and keep business. The other men noticed the newcomer but pretended to pay him no mind, concentrating instead on the game. Some of them may have been among the crowd that had seen him ride in with Jessie. Ki ordered some coffee and tinned fruit.

The store owner bustled around the counter to fetch the items. "You just passing through, mister?" he asked casually. But it was apparent to Ki that he was masking a genuine interest. New folks in Beacon were rare, especially tall Orientals who moved with quiet power and spoke softly and whose eyes took in everything.

"I may be around for a few days," Ki answered.

"My name is Tom Archer," the shopkeeper said, extending a fleshy, callused hand.

Ki took his hand. "I am Ki."

"You know, I can't help noticing, Mr. Ki, that you're only wearing that little knife there by way of protection. Just a word of friendly advice—this here town gets pretty wild sometimes, and some folks keep an eye out for strangers, just wanting to cause trouble. Don't aim to put a bad face on Beacon, and I ain't saying you can't handle yourself— but I thought I'd mention it. No need for you to walk into something and get yourself hurt."

"Thank you, Mr. Archer. I'll keep that in mind. How much do I owe you for the provisions?"

Archer totaled up the bill and Ki paid, but the shopkeeper went on, "So where do you come from, Mr. Ki?" He leaned against the counter, resting his ample weight there and looking directly at his strange customer.

"Texas," Ki replied. "My employer and I live in Texas."

"Now that's a mighty far piece from Beacon, Nebraska. Would I be imposing on you too much to ask you why you and him came all the way up here from Texas?"

"Yes," said Ki.

"Look, no offense," Archer protested. "It's just that we get so few strangers in town these days. Most folks is on

100

their way out. In fact, we may all be on our way, day after tomorrow."

Feigning ignorance, Ki asked, "Why the day after tomorrow?"

"Haven't you heard? That's the day of the big fight. Our man, Dale Knowlton, is gonna whup the carny man. Leastways we hope so, 'cause if not, we lose everything we've got." Archer explained the situation: The carnival management was putting up ten thousand dollars against nearly every square inch of property in Beacon—and the townspeople had taken the bet, pinning their thin hopes on the young blacksmith.

"If anybody can do it, Knowlton can," Archer went on. "And if he don't, hell, we lose it all—but that ain't much worse than what's happening now. Beacon's ready to die anyhow."

Dale Knowlton was the man Jessie was seeking, Ki realized, wondering if she had found him by now. But he prodded Archer: "Why is that?"

"See, we had great hopes that the railroad company would build a spur out this way. In fact, they kept promising us they would—until about two years ago, when they finally turned us down flat. That was the writing on the wall, and folks started moving out. Some of us stayed, and we tried to build up the town. But, you see, there's no money coming in. The few farmers and cattlemen around ain't making enough to meet expenses. There ain't no hotels to speak of anymore—just one fleabag above another fella's saloon out yonder. And saloons take up all a man's spending money hereabouts. I'm just barely keeping my own place together. There's nothing to keep us here other than our businesses. So I guess we all figured we might as well gamble for some money to keep us going—or else move on."

So these folks didn't know of Kelso's so-called discovery, Ki thought. They had given up hope, thinking they had nothing to lose but the little they possessed. It wasn't a gutless decision, if Archer could be believed, but the only realistic one. They were people with no future, in a town ready to go under. He could understand that, and yet the injustice of the situation was glaring. The townspeople had no idea they were sitting on a possible oil field—a way out for them—and no one was telling them, least of all Goodpaster.

Ki nodded gravely. He placed the provisions in the saddlebag and slung it over his shoulder. "I hope your man wins, Mr. Archer."

"I do too, Mr. Ki. I've kinda taken a liking to this place. I don't know where else I'd go."

As he stepped outside, Ki wondered if Jessie had found out what was happening. He imagined she had, somehow. And she was probably asking herself the same question he was pondering—what did Wallace Winslow have to do with this setup, along with Goodpaster, the carnival owner, who had sent his hired men out to ambush them? He felt the soft dust of the street beneath his cotton shoes. How did it all connect? Could oil, or whatever Kelso had found, mean that much to these men?

Already more than a few men had died for it, and that included Kelso himself. Ki realized that more men would die before it was over.

Across the street he heard the noise from a saloon, the one Archer had pointed out. It was the cacophony of men drinking and gambling and easing their minds from the problems that plagued them daily. Ki figured the saloon would be a good place to feel the pulse of the town.

The shabby front of the building and the unpainted batwing doors notwithstanding, the place was crowded with men. Ki counted at least twenty in the cramped, smoky room. Several were at the bar to the right of the entrance, hunched over their drinks and chatting among themselves. The others sat at the few wobbly tables that took up the rest of the space in the saloon, playing cards or talking idly and drinking with abandon. As Archer had said, in bad times like these a saloon was the only profitable business around; men will always drink, even if they and their families go hungry to pay for it.

Ki edged up to the end of the bar closest to the door. He put the saddlebag down near the rail that ran along the bottom of the cheaply constructed pineboard bar. The surface was stained with spilled drinks and sweat and body grease from the men who lived at it. As he waited for the bartender to serve him, Ki caught the men glancing in his direction, one by one, taking note of his presence among them.

They kept talking as if nothing unusual were happening, but the stranger felt that he was being inspected by the smelly, rough-hewn regulars who would have to be curious as to who he was. Unlike the direct, plain-talking shopkeeper, Archer, these men were taciturn and suspicious. If any one of them cared to confront Ki, it would take him a while to get around to it—maybe another drink or two. But Ki was in no hurry. He caught the barkeep's eye. The man ambled over, his shoulders bent and his face craggy.

"Yeah?" he said.

"You have cold beer?" Ki asked.

"Nope. Nothin' cold in this town—'cept the women-folk."

"I'll take a whiskey, then."

"Beer's tolerable good, even if'n it ain't 'zactly cold."

"Thank you, but I'll still take whiskey."

"If'n that's yer poison . . ." the man mumbled as he fetched a bottle and poured Ki a glassful. "You want me to leave the bottle?" he asked, pushing the drink across the bar.

"No, I'll work on this one for now."

"That'll be two bits. And it's worth it, 'cause it ain't watered down none."

Ki paid him and brought the glass to his lips. The outside of the glass was greasy to the touch. He guessed the bartender didn't have time to wash the glasses. The man to Ki's left turned to face him, watching as he took his first sip. Ki winced; the whiskey was awful, even if it wasn't watered. It was worse than the cheapest *sake* in a country tavern in Japan.

"Powerful bad stupid water," said the man standing next to Ki. He was obviously very drunk, weaving back and forth, his tie unknotted, his suit wrinkled. He wore a battered, dusty derby hat and his face was mottled and unshaven. He looked in bad shape. But he smiled, giving Ki a view of his stained and yellowing teeth.

"Perhaps I should have ordered warm beer," Ki said.

"Worse," the drunk advised, shaking his head. "I know for a fact he pisses into the beer barrels when he's drunk— which is every night. He thinks it's funny."

"Thank you for the advice," Ki acknowledged.

"Hell, that's what I'm best at—giving good advice. Never learned how to take it, myself. But I can dispense it with the best of them. Allow me to present myself. J. Henry Ettinger, attorney at law. Most folks—those who speak to me—call me Hank."

Ki smiled, his dark eyes sparkling. A lawyer, and a drunk one at that. Here was a man who might be able to tell him more about Beacon. He introduced himself and took another drink of the godawful whiskey. The second swallow didn't taste quite as bad as the first.

"The more you drink, the more tolerable it gets," Ettinger commented. "And after six or seven drinks, it tastes positively passable." He put a thumb to his breast. "You're talking to an expert." He slugged down the rest of his own drink and slammed the glass down on the scarred bar. The barkeep slouched over. "I'll have another, Ted, and one for my friend here."

Ted's eyes trailed the edge of the bar as he said in a low voice, "But Mr. Ettinger, I told you, your credit's no good no more. I believe in charity, but I done charitied you long enough. I'm sorry." He turned to go away, but Ettinger reached over the bar and grabbed his sleeve.

"By God, Ted!" he roared. "You aim to humiliate me here in front of my friend? You know I'm good for it at the end of the month. When haven't I paid you—you—"

The bartender wrenched himself from Ettinger's grasp. "Golly damn, none of us is gonna *be here* at the end of the month. I can't afford to wait till then."

"You don't think our valiant champion will win this illegal and immoral wager for our very souls?" Ettinger demanded theatrically. "You've already given up the ghost, Ted. Well, I have not—not yet. So I want another drink!" His pale face flushed with anger and frustration. He surely didn't need another drink. But he was adamant.

Ted turned to Ki with an uncertain look, wondering if the Oriental was going to join Ettinger in the argument. The other men at the bar ignored the set-to, as if it were a normal occurrence.

Ki said, "I'll pay. Get Mr. Ettinger a drink."

As the barkeep slunk away, the lawyer turned to his new-found friend. "I'll be forever grateful to you for this, Mr. Ki. Forever grateful. That is," he added with a sly wink, "if I remember what happened in the morning. It is the curse of the drinking man that his memory becomes somewhat useless. I always remember to promise myself, 'Never again,' but I soon forget even that vow, and by sunset—oftentimes much sooner—I'm back here again, at Ted's mercy. Be that as it may, I thank you again."

By this time Ted had returned with a bottle. Ettinger raised it to Ki's health and took a generous swig directly from the bottle.

The other saloon patrons continued, unaware of this small drama in their midst, to keep the hapless Ted hopping. Ki was amazed at the amount of liquor being consumed. These men, like Ettinger, wanted to forget, to erase the specter of their bargain with the devil, to put out of their minds the death of their town. Ki wondered how they could have agreed to such an insane proposition. Yet, to see them, to see the town of Beacon, was to realize that they had given up all hope long ago. Now they had the chance to have their fate decided for them; thus they could claim they were not responsible for the decision.

Ettinger, though, seemed to show a spark of fight still. Maybe he drank more than the rest of them, but he obviously had some intelligence left in him.

The lawyer condescended to pour whiskey in his glass. He placed the bottle between Ki and himself. "Doesn't taste too bad. Better than none at all, eh?"

Ki decided to have another. Whenever he drank, he maintained the same discipline as he did in the rest of his life. Knowing his limits, and knowing that other men expected him to drink with them, he took it slow and steady. He knew what drink could do to a man; he had seen too many like Hank Ettinger.

"I'm interested," said Ki, still admitting no knowledge about the situation, "in learning about this illegal and immoral wager, Mr. Ettinger."

The attorney chuckled, reaching into his coat. He pulled out a folded paper and tossed it to Ki. "Read that. I'll be damned if it doesn't tell the whole sordid story of this gutless town."

Ki unfolded it. It was the same notice he and Jessie had seen posted all over town, announcing the fight the day after tomorrow. He read it over again and turned to Ettinger. "The people have agreed to this? They're risking everything for ten thousand dollars?"

"Indeed they have, sir. Ignoble and ignorant as it sounds. The so-called good people of Beacon have given up on themselves. I salute them in their last days as men." The lawyer raised his whiskey glass in a mock toast.

"You say it's not legal," Ki noted.

"Of course it's not," Ettinger replied. "The town is chartered by the state, and only the state can revoke that charter. But when I told them that, they wouldn't listen. All they can see is that ten thousand dollars—which will never appear. This man Goodpaster is bound and determined to take over Beacon—God only knows why. And most of the folks here are only too glad to give it over to him. Or else collect their share of the prize money and get drunk with it."

"You don't have a town marshal who can stop this business?"

"Nope. Chet Barkley was our marshal. He up and died of a bullet in the back over a year ago. No one else has volunteered for the job. The nearest law is the sheriff in Gilead. But he has all of Box Butte County to cover—and he's none too good at his job."

"I've met him," said Ki.

"Then you know what I mean. I suppose I'm as close as anything to a lawman in these parts, being sworn as an officer of the court, such as it is. The circuit judge rarely comes around anymore." He poured another glassful of the ripe whiskey. "They drafted me to act as referee in the ring, day after tomorrow. Been reading up on my Marquis of Queensberry rules." He waved a tattered booklet that he retrieved from his pocket. "Doesn't make any difference, though. These carnival people have Beacon's neck in a noose. They're just waiting to pull it tight. You going to be around for the hanging?"

"Yes, I'll be there," Ki said. He put some money on the bar and collected his saddlebag. "Good to meet you, Mr. Ettinger."

"You're not leaving—it's early yet. Have one more drink. Hell, you bought it."

"I've had enough for one night."

"Well, thanks for bailing me out. I'll repay you as soon as I can," the attorney promised.

"No need for that. Glad to help out."

Ettinger lifted his hand in a shaky salute. "You sleep

well, Mr. Ki. And if I can ever be of service, please do not hesitate to call upon me."

"I won't," said Ki.

On his way back to the telegraph office, Ki sensed trouble before he saw anything. The narrow streets of Beacon were dark, unlighted. Most folks were in for the night, with their shutters drawn. Ki looked cautiously over his right shoulder. He saw two figures behind him, about a block distant. They were singing and staggering along the plankwalk as if drunk. But the samurai had seen this trick before. He continued walking, picking up the pace slightly.

When he looked back a minute later, he saw that they were keeping up with him. Then, quickly, he turned into a narrow alleyway just across the street from the livery where he'd stabled the horses. He pulled up and looked around the corner. He saw them. There was no stagger in their stride now; they were running full speed toward the alley.

Dropping the saddlebag, Ki lifted a nearby water barrel and stepped to the mouth of the alley. Just as the two bushwhackers approached him, he heaved the barrel at them. It caught one man full in the chest and sent him to the ground with a grunt that knocked the wind out of him. The second man jumped over his fallen comrade and came at Ki.

The samurai ran five yards and spun suddenly. Now he was facing the oncoming man, who had his revolver drawn. Feinting to the right and then to the left, Ki avoided the first shot. He dove as the man triggered a second round at nearly point-blank range. The bullet split the air only inches from Ki's head. Keeping low, balancing on one hand and one foot, Ki brought his other foot around in a wide arc, sweeping the man's legs out from under him. The man crashed to the ground, flat on his back.

Ki then leaped to his feet and deftly kicked the sixgun

from the stranger's hand. The man shook his head and looked around to see what had hit him. Ki stood there, less than ten feet away. The man scrambled to his feet, found his gun hand empty, and charged. Ki sidestepped the lunging bushwhacker, bringing both hands down hard on the man's back, chopping him face-down into the dirt.

The man rolled away, regained his balance, and got up again. He stood at least six feet tall, and his long arms were poised for action. Catching his breath, he circled Ki widely. The two men kept their eyes on each other. Ki faked a head-on attack; the other jumped away. Ki rocked back, giving ground. The bushwhacker saw his chance. Reaching behind his back, he drew a hidden knife as he ran at Ki.

Ki stood with his legs spread, concentrating his power in his hands, centering his spirit on the attacker. He saw the knife glint dully, and ducked when it swept over his head as the man tried to slash his face.

No one had come out at the sound of the two shots. Ki knew he couldn't expect any help from the townsfolk. And out of the corner of his eye he saw the downed man stirring. He moved a half-step to the attacker's left, away from the knife hand.

The alley was almost totally enveloped in darkness, but Ki could see the glint of killing light in the man's eyes as he brandished the blade. With one swift step the man was upon Ki, the knife slashing within inches of the samurai's face. Ki ducked beneath the swinging arm and bolted deeper into the alleyway. He turned then and unsheathed his own *ko-dachi* blade, balancing it carefully, lightly in his hand.

Against the dim light from the street he saw two silhouettes, the one with the knife closer, the other slowly approaching. Ki felt something at his back as he retreated even farther—it was a dead end. For once, he cursed his *karma*. Already today, he and Jessie had been forced to do some unpleasant killing. Now Ki was in the same position once again. He was sick of it. How, he wondered, could so many men be so violent, so heedless of life? He steeled himself to the task at hand.

Holding the *ko-dachi* firmly by the razor-sharp blade, he calculated the distance and velocity required. Generally he did not use the knife for throwing, not liking it to leave his hand unnecessarily. But this time it was his best bet. The man, figuring to have Ki hopelessly cornered, came on. With a whip-quick turn of his wrist, the samurai released his own knife. He heard the man cry out in shock and pain, saw the black shadow fall. If he had hit his target properly, the *ko-dachi* was buried in the attacker's breast.

The second man stopped short, not knowing what was happening to his companion. Ki jumped over the downed man and made his way toward the alley mouth. The second man could not see him coming. Ki lunged at him, pushing him to the ground. The man recovered and wrapped his arms around Ki as they grappled together, rolling into the wall of a building. Ki managed to push the man off, freeing himself from the death grip. He leaped to his feet and assumed the classic *te* fighting stance, his elbows bent, his hands upraised.

The man shook his head and slid up against the wall, bracing himself and easing upright. He was prepared for another head-on assault, but Ki fooled him. The samurai spun on his right foot, lifting his left leg high. The quick, expert movement caught the man off guard. In fact, Ki moved so fast that an ordinary man could see him only as a blur. The left foot came around, slamming into the side of the man's head, stunning him. Ki followed with a lightning-quick smash to the attacker's face with his open hand. He felt the man's nose flatten and blood start to flow.

Ki did not let him fall; instead, he eased the man down and placed his knee at the man's throat. Stunned, his face painfully smashed, the bushwhacker's eyes were wide open with fear. He didn't know what to expect from the half-Japanese warrior.

110

Tired of asking the same question, Ki said, "Who sent you?"

"No—nobody," the man gasped.

"Why did you attack me?"

"We just—we was havin' fun. Thought maybe you had some money—that's all, mister."

"Where are you from?"

"Right here—Beacon," the man said, blood running from his broken nose into his mouth. "Honest—we was just—we didn't mean no harm."

"You caused harm enough. Your friend is hurt badly."

"Don't feel so good myself," the man replied sheepishly.

"You are not dead. You are lucky."

Ki felt angry enough to finish both of them off, but he believed the man's story. It was just a stupid coincidence that they had chosen to assault him. They were obviously two bumbling thieves who had picked on the wrong victim. He shoved the man aside and went to retrieve his *ko-dachi* blade. The first man was still breathing. He would lose a lot of blood and would be in shock for while, but he'd live. The other would live too, with a rearranged face.

The samurai left them there to lick their wounds. His own hands were bloody, so he wiped them on one of the men's shirts. Then he picked up his saddlebag and went to the telegraph office, where the telegraph clerk had stuck to their bargain and had kept the place open until Ki returned.

From behind a pair of thick spectacles, the man looked at Ki's crimson hands and took a long, hard swallow. Sweat beaded on his pink forehead. "Got your message, Mr. Ki," he croaked.

"Thank you. Here's an extra dollar." Ki tossed him a silver cartwheel. "Where is the message?"

"Right, here you go." The telegraph operator passed Ki a yellow sheet of paper.

Ki glanced at the message and thanked the man again. He left, the man's eyes still glued to his hands. At a nearby water trough, Ki washed the blood off. That felt better. He then made his way to the site where he and Jessie had agreed to meet, near the railroad station. She was there, along with a very tall young man.

"Did you run into any trouble, Ki?" she asked him, with concern in her eyes.

"I had some trouble," the samurai said noncommittally. "Have you waited long for me?"

"No, Dale and I got here just a few minutes ago. Ki, this is Dale Knowlton, Mr. Kelso's friend. Dale, my partner, Ki."

The two men shook hands, sizing each other up with a glance. Ki trusted his first impressions of men, and Knowlton impressed him fine. Dale, too, took no longer than a few seconds to decide that Ki was a capable fighting man, worthy of Jessie's trust and friendship.

"Pleased to meet you, Ki," he said.

Ki nodded in acknowledgment. He turned to Jessie and said, "The Omaha marshal's office answered our telegraph message." He handed her the reply.

Jessie read it, a cloud of apprehension gathering in her mind. The message in the telegraph clerk's spidery hand-writing was terse but informative:

JULIUS GOODPASTER ALIAS OF JAMES G. CAMPBELL WANTED BY U S AUTHORITIES FOR GRAND LARCENY AND BANK FRAUD IN OHIO MISSOURI AND KANSAS STOP SUSPECT OF SCOTTISH BIRTH WITH CRIMINAL RECORD IN THAT COUNTRY HAS CONTACTS IN CANADA MEXICO AND EUROPE STOP CONSIDERED DANGEROUS KNOWN TO HAVE KILLED SIX MEN INCLUDING TWO LAW OFFICERS STOP

"Doesn't paint a pretty picture of our Mr. J.G., does it?" she muttered. She passed the message to Dale. He read it and swore. "You think he's prepared to pay Beacon ten thousand dollars if his man loses tomorrow?" she asked the blacksmith.

"The son of a bitch *better* pay up."

"He pays his backshooters, that's for sure," said Jessie.

Ki said, "He wants us out of the way. With this, we know too much."

"I won't let him touch you," Knowlton promised.

"Thanks, Dale, but Goodpaster himself won't get his hands dirty. He'll hire men—plenty of men—to do the job for him. We've already fought off some of them. There'll be more, though. Unless we can get to Goodpaster, or Campbell or whatever his name is, first."

"How, Jessie?" asked Ki.

"I don't have a single damned idea," she said.

"If he's going to all this trouble over Beacon," Knowlton said, "he must think the place is worth having."

"For the oil Kelso found, or for something," Jessie said. "He can't know there's anything here, though, until it's brought out of the ground. He's gambling on a big strike."

"Perhaps he knows more than we do," Ki suggested.

"How'd he find out?" Jessie wondered. "Only Kelso did all the studying and research. He knew more than anybody."

"Somehow Goodpaster found out enough to make him real interested," Knowlton said.

Jessie was tired. The battle on the trail, the ride into Beacon, the lovemaking with Dale—and now this new corridor in a never-ending maze. It all made even less sense than before. Goodpaster, with his international connections—she didn't like it a bit.

"I'll see you tomorrow morning, Jessie," said Knowlton.

"Good night, Dale." She watched him go, his massive frame absorbed by the darkness. "Let's fetch our bedrolls and grab some shut-eye, Ki. This has been a killing day."

Ki did not smile at her unintended joke. He knew some grim business lay ahead in the next day or two—more killing days. The only question was, who'd do the killing—and who'd do the dying?

★

Chapter 7

The next day Jessie agreed to accompany Dale to the site outside of town where he had been training for the fight. She rode beside the silent blacksmith in an old buckboard pulled by two big mares. He told her he'd show her something she'd be interested in out there, but he didn't elaborate further. She rested on the ride out, letting the sun bake her face and warm her inside and out. Being with Dale was a nice enough way, she decided, to spend a morning—away, for a while, from the troubling and volatile situation in Beacon.

The place was an abandoned farmhouse some three miles north of Beacon. No telling how long it had been since people had lived there. Even Dale, who knew as much as anyone in Beacon about the folks who lived and worked around the town, wasn't sure.

"Small family, I figure," he said. "The house has two

bedrooms and a small kitchen. They didn't even finish the barn. That's where I've been training."

He led her to the uncompleted barn. Three walls and a part of the fourth had been erected, and the beams of the roof had been raised. In one corner, Knowlton had built a shelf that sheltered that area from direct sunlight. And hanging there was a long, heavy bag made of an army-issue horsehair blanket stuffed with straw. Dale called it a "punching bag," and he demonstrated how he used it.

Stripping to the waist, the tall young blacksmith danced around the bag, peppering it with punches as if it were his opponent in the boxing ring. After several minutes of this, he steadied the bag and paused to catch his breath.

"I read about it in *The Police Gazette*. Some of the professional prizefighters use this method of training. They also hire men to fight with them in a practice ring—they call them sparring partners. Can you imagine sparring with John L. Sullivan? I sure can't."

"Dale," Jessie said, "are you certain you'll be ready to fight Heany? I mean, it's a good thing you've been training like this, but he's been fighting for years. He knows a lot more about the game than you do."

Knowlton smiled. "It's nice that you care about me, Jessie. But don't worry, I can handle myself. It'll be Heany who regrets this match, not me. I'm fighting for more than just money."

Jessie shook her head. "You're a stubborn one," she declared.

"I'll bet I'm not more stubborn than you." He came and put his arms around her, his wide chest glistening with perspiration, his handsome face just inches from hers. "You usually get what you want, don't you?"

"I suppose I do," she conceded with a laugh.

Knowlton worked out for an hour, punching the bag and executing a series of exercises that he said strengthened certain parts of his body and helped maintain endurance.

He rested and drank some water before limbering up for another half hour. Jessie watched with fascination. Dale Knowlton was as close to a perfect specimen physically as she had ever seen. Even Custis Long, the deputy U.S. marshal who was never far from her thoughts, didn't have as finely trim a body as Dale—and Longarm was a damned attractive man. Enough of that, she chided herself—no use comparing the two men. She very much liked them both....

His big shadow blocked off the sun, startling her out of her ruminations. "You hungry?" he asked. She was, and they proceeded to break open the picnic lunch she had packed for them.

Dale finished off a bottle of water, pouring the last few ounces over his head to cool himself off. She laughed and threw him a clean cotton towel with which he wiped his face. The basket contained some cold chicken and potato salad and bread and butter. Jessie had even bought a jar of strawberry jam for the bread.

"Well, I'm ready for this," the blacksmith said, rubbing his giant hands together. "If it tastes half as good as you did last night, I'll eat it all up."

"Dale! You're getting less and less shy, I guess—making me blush!" Indeed, her creamy cheeks reddened at his comparison. It surprised her somewhat, but she liked what he said.

"Well, it's the truth," he mumbled, realizing how his intended compliment had come out. "Even if I did say it kind of crude."

"There's nothing crude about you, Dale," Jessie reassured him. "You're a gentleman through and through. A girl appreciates that in a man. As well as a naughty joke or two in private."

He kissed her. "I have three reasons to fight, now: the town, revenge against Heany, and you. Will you be in my corner tomorrow, Jessie? I'd like you to be there."

"Ki and I both will be," she said. "I want to be sure it's

a fair fight. They may try to steal it from you. I won't let them get away with it."

"Hell, I plan to get in there and beat the bastard up. Fair and square."

"If confidence can win the fight, he hasn't got a chance."

"Pass that chicken leg over here, ma'am," he said, stuffing a piece of bread in his mouth.

When they were finished eating, Jessie asked him, "What was it that you were going to show me? Something you said I'd be interested in."

Knowlton stood and put his shirt back on. Helping her to her feet, he embraced her again. They kissed. The blacksmith felt the hot iron of need in the furnace of his loins. He wanted to take her right there, in the abandoned barn, and make love to her again and again. But he knew he must be cautious, and conserve energy for the fight.

"Come on, I'll show you," he said. He took her about a hundred yards from the barn, to a low gully through which a sluggish stream made its progress. He bent down to the stream and came up with a handful of water. Opening his fingers, he allowed the water to drain out. A filmy substance remained on his hand.

Jessie touched the substance and tasted a bit of it. "Oil," she said.

"This is where Kelso was working, doing his surveying and such. He wanted to drill a well over there." Dale pointed to a flat, open piece of land to the left of the gully.

"He wanted *you* to drill him a well, you mean."

"Yeah, that's why he ordered the equipment. Like I told you, I'd build the drill following his directions. He said he had read all about how to do it, and he'd work with me on it."

"And are you sure you're the only one he spoke to? Why would Winslow, or this man who calls himself Goodpaster, know as much as they do?"

"I wouldn't put anything past Winslow. From what Kelso told me, the man's a sneaky son of a bitch. I don't know about Goodpaster, except that he wants to take over the whole town—and this land here."

"I wonder..." Jessie thought aloud. "Goodpaster isn't what he seems, if the Omaha U.S. marshal's office is right. Winslow, too, might not be who he claims. Who's pulling the strings?" She couldn't get the question out of her head, but for now she put it aside. "How much petroleum did Kelso think he'd be able to bring up?" she asked Knowlton.

"Never said specific. See, that's the trouble, Jessie. Kelso said too much and not enough. Maybe he wasn't clear about it himself. Just guessing."

"Damned good guessing, at that," she said.

"Yeah. But it didn't do him any good."

Jessie kicked a toeful of dirt out of the bottom of the sandy gully. "No, it didn't. But he hasn't been forgotten."

She went out to look over the proposed drilling location. She marveled at the thought that there might be barrels and barrels of black petroleum under the ground where she stood. From what she knew of the process, it would take lots of hard work to bring it up and ship it out. Like the men down in the Indian Territory and Texas who were drilling and refining the stuff, she wondered if the Starbuck company could locate even a small reserve here, improbably, in Nebraska. It could mean a good piece of change. Yes, it was worth exploring, and she was grateful to Kelso for being as farsighted as he was.

She turned to the blacksmith. "Dale, we're fighting for a lot more here than one broken-down old town."

"I know that," he said. "And when it's over, Jessie—"

Jessie put a finger on his lips. "Let's not start making plans too far in advance. One day at a time is tough enough."

"Sure," he said. "Don't count your chickens and all that stuff."

"It's true, you know. You've got to fight Heany. I've got to fight Winslow and Goodpaster. We both have our hands full."

Knowlton opened his big, work-hardened blacksmith's hands. Jessie saw the scars and calluses that testified to the man's years of labor at the forge. "My hands aren't nearly as full as I want them to be. After tomorrow I'll help you, Jessie. My hands are ready to take on some of your work. That is, if you'll let me."

"Damn it, Dale," she breathed. "If you keep offering, I may let you."

He smiled, looking down into her clear emerald eyes, wanting so much to take her away from this place and keep her out of harm's reach. "I'll hold you to that, gal."

She lifted her lips to his and they kissed again, his strong embrace crushing her against him. For a brief moment they were alone in their private world, sparked by memories of the night before. But the whickering of Dale's mares brought them back to reality.

Jessie reacted instantly, lifting her converted .38 Colt revolver from the cordovan holster at her hip. She pivoted away from Knowlton. "Did you hear that?"

"Yeah," Dale said. He was unarmed.

"Where's your rifle?" Jessie asked.

He realized then what he had done. "I left it in the boot on the wagon."

"Damn," she cursed. She followed him back to the gully. They moved silently, warily. They found a spot from which they could see the barn. There was no sign of intruders.

"I don't see anybody," the blacksmith said.

"No, but I'd feel a darn sight better if I knew for sure why those horses are upset." As she spoke, the animals whinnied once again, with more urgency this time. This riled her. "Why did we leave them unprotected? Why were we so blamed careless?"

"Don't go badmouthing yourself, Jessie. I'm the one left

120

his gun at the wagon. If anything happens to you because of me—"

Jessie squeezed his arm lightly. "Nothing's going to happen, Dale." But inside she felt differently; there was something going on here that she did not like in the least.

Together they climbed out of the gully and took cover behind a nearby stand of trees, about sixty yards from the barn. This gave them a closer look, but they did not see anything new. Whoever was out there wasn't making a visible movement or a sound. Jessie and Knowlton grew impatient, but they knew better than to make any sudden, thoughtless moves for the barn—as long as they did not know who, and how many, were out there.

Several minutes passed—and still there was nothing. Jessie whispered to Knowlton, "It's no good just waiting here. But I don't know what else to do."

Knowlton thought for a minute. "I could circle around through those trees there, and try to get at the wagon. If I get hold of my rifle, at least we're both armed. You stay here and keep out of sight. Whoever is out there likely doesn't know how many of us there are."

"I don't like it, Dale. There's too much open ground between here and the wagon. What if there are three of four men out there? You wouldn't stand a chance."

"You know, it could just be some harmless kid out in the woods who came on the barn and the wagon. It could be nothing." But he didn't convince himself, much less Jessie.

"Don't bet on it." She was reluctant to see him go, but there was probably no other way.

Knowlton kissed her on the cheek and started off. Keeping to the cover of every available tree, he skirted the abandoned barn. There was no one in sight, but he could hear his two mares stamping and snorting, as if a stranger were holding them. The idea made him angry; who the hell was sneaking up on them, and why? Crouching low and moving as silently as possible, he progressed another twenty feet, finally reaching the far side of the barn.

There he saw the man standing at the wagon, calming the animals. The man was armed with a long-barreled rifle and a brace of revolvers slung from a gunbelt at his waist. A low-crowned, bent-brimmed hat shadowed his features, and he kept looking around, either to catch sight of a partner or to locate the animals' owner.

Knowlton was some ten yards away in the trees and undergrowth, invisible but virtually helpless. But he decided the only way out was to attack the man at the wagon and somehow recover his own gun. He took a deep breath and waited for his chance.

The stranger remained on the alert. Then Knowlton had an idea. He found a small rock and gauged the distance he'd need to throw it. Lifting himself on his haunches, he lofted the rock over the animal's heads; it landed in the dust just a few feet from them. As he had hoped, this disturbed the horses and distracted the man's attention.

In one leaping movement, the young blacksmith was on his feet and racing toward the wagon. Coming at the man from behind, Knowlton tackled him, sending the rifle clattering to the ground. The man himself went down with a surprised grunt, and the horses whinnied and backed away. Dale felt the man struggling beneath him. He unleashed a smashing blow to the back of the man's head, which crashed facedown into the dust.

Knowlton scrambled to his feet and went around to the driver's side of the wagon where he kept his rifle. It was gone. He looked about frantically. Where the hell—? Then, in desperation, he bent to pick up the fallen man's gun. For insurance, he went over to the man to disarm him. He tossed one revolver into the brush and reached for the other.

Just then he felt a boot in his side. The pain drove through him and sent him sprawling. He struggled to catch his breath, but before he could, another boot planted itself in his gut, right below the ribs. It nearly made him vomit as he flailed his arms to ward off another blow. None came. Someone reached down and turned him over on his back.

Knowlton looked up into the mocking faces of two men who had him lined up in their rifle sights.

"Get up, big man," one of them said. He was a tall, slender, dark-skinned man with long black hair—looked like a half-breed. He held a black-barreled Henry repeating rifle on the blacksmith.

The other was a short man with a large head, long in need of a shave, and he wore a yellow bandanna. He carried what looked to be a Colt .36 revolving rifle. Knowlton hadn't seen one of those in a long time.

As Dale got to his feet, the half-breed spoke again. "Where's the woman, Knowlton?"

"What woman?" As the words escaped his lips, he knew he had said the wrong thing. The shorter man's rifle barrel came cracking across Knowlton's face. It hit him on the right cheekbone, slashing open the skin. Knowlton slumped to his knees, his hand coming up to his cut cheek.

"I'll only ask once more," the half-breed said coldly. "Where is she?"

The blacksmith was riled. He didn't like threats—from any man. He regarded the half-breed's black eyes stoically and spit a juicy wad of saliva that landed inches from the man's boots.

The shorter man again brought his rifle barrel around. Dale tried to block it with his powerful hands. But the man drew back the barrel and used the butt to smack Knowlton's hand away. He then drove the butt into the young man's gut, doubling him over. With his knee, the blue-eyed man jolted Knowlton's mouth shut and brought him back erect, reeling. Blood flowed out of the corners of Dale's lips and his head rang with pain and confusion. He wondered if Jessie had caught wind of his troubles by now, and he hoped she'd stay far away and not get mixed up in this. If he could keep these hardcases occupied for a while, she could escape and get back to town, to her friend Ki.

The man Knowlton had downed was stirring now, shaking his head and spitting dirt out of his mouth. He looked around to see the blacksmith wincing in pain and the half-breed glaring at him, saying, "Enjoy your nap?"

Staggering upright, the man instinctively checked his sidearms, and found one missing. He glared at Knowlton. "Where'd it go?" he asked.

"Yonder," Dale managed, nodding his head in the direction he'd thrown the revolver, wishing the man would somehow break his neck on the way over to look for it.

"You still haven't told me what I want to know," the half-breed addressed Knowlton through clenched teeth. "I hadn't ought to give you another chance, but I'm feeling generous—so one more chance, Mr. Blacksmith."

A pistol shot cracked the still air. A grunt came from the man who was looking for his gun, and he fell—a bullet having severed his spine. The two others swung around, their rifles at the ready. A drifting cloud of gunsmoke at one corner of the barn was the only sign of the gunman— or, in this case, gun*woman*—so the two hardcases held their fire.

The half-breed turned his Henry rifle on Dale Knowlton. "It's not going to work," he muttered. "Either she comes out and gives up, or you're a dead man."

"You think I care?" Dale challenged him.

"Big talk. You'll die slow—and she'll watch. I don't reckon she wants that."

The man had a point. Jessie wouldn't let Knowlton die in front of her eyes—not if she could do anything to prevent it. But Knowlton kept quiet.

"Listen up, girl!" called Steel Knife, his eyes not flickering from the blacksmith. "Your man is dead if you don't give yourself up. I don't care that much about him; it's you we want. You want to see him die, we'll be obliged to let

124

you. But there's no need for it if you come out."

Silence greeted his words. Dale wondered what Jessie was up to. There was really no way out for him, but he still wanted her to make a run for it. "You're wasting your breath," he told the half-breed.

"I don't think so." He moved around behind Knowlton, the end of his rifle barrel planted squarely in his victim's back, so that he could see the barn. His partner kept his gun aimed in that direction too.

Suddenly Jessie's voice rang out, breaking the tense stillness of the confrontation. "What do you want from us?" she called.

The stern-faced half-breed made a sound that might be taken for a grim laugh. "Nothing much. Just show your face and drop your weapon. Then we can talk, friendly-like."

"You're acting none too friendly," Jessie retorted. "Let Dale go and I'll come out."

"No dice, lady. Our orders are to take you both—alive if we can, the other way if we have to."

"Whose orders are you taking?"

"Easy enough for you to find out. Just throw down your gun and we'll talk about it."

"Don't do it, Jessie!" Knowlton's plea was cut short as the shorter man cracked him on the jaw once again with his gunbarrel. The big blacksmith went down in a heap, his mind curtained in blackness. Now both hardcases held their rifles at the ready, waiting.

Jessie saw the whole thing from her position behind the half-built wall of the barn. When Knowlton went down again, she winced. That decided her. She cursed inwardly. How had she gotten into this mess—and dragged Dale in with her?

Holding her revolver over her head, she came around from behind the barn. She tossed the gun out in front of her. As she strode out to meet them, her fiery red-gold hair blew in the hot breeze. She saw their faces and swore to herself that she'd next see them in hell. . . .

Blindfolded and hogtied, Jessie and Knowlton rode in the back of the wagon. Tied behind it was the dead man's horse with its owner's corpse draped across the saddle. In front, the two kidnappers led the wagon over the rugged terrain. Dale soon woke up, his head throbbing. And both of the prisoners, as the wagon jostled and jolted them, felt the severe discomfort of their bonds.

They traveled for over two hours like this, and Jessie could not tell which direction they were going. All she knew was that she was angry as hell at herself for dragging Dale into this situation. How stupid not to be properly armed at all times, not to be alert and ready for anything! Hadn't her father and Ki warned her repeatedly against the possibility of being caught unawares, and taught her how to guard against it?

It was too late now for self-recriminations. The next step was to figure out how to get away, or to get word to Ki of their predicament. Even to discover their destination was next to impossible, since they were blindfolded. Still, she wouldn't give up hope—not yet.

When the wagon stopped, Jessie could sense that they were in the midst of a large camp—with several more men and animals about. She smelled fires burning, and horseshit and grass. There was little or no protection from the sun. Their captors spoke in hushed tones among themselves. Then Jessie and Knowlton were trundled off the wagon. They were deposited in what felt like a small box, or perhaps another wagon. She heard the sound of a padlock clicking on the door outside. Then the men moved away and left the two of them alone.

"Dale?" she whispered. "Are you hurt bad?"

The blacksmith groaned. "I feel like I've been pounded by one of my own hammers. But I'll live. And I'll kill those sons of bitches with my own hands. Jessie, I'm sorry I got us into this."

"It wasn't you, Dale. We were both pretty stupid. We'll get out somehow."

Inside the box, the air was stale and fetid. She could feel his big body close to her. The ropes around her arms, legs, and wrists bit into her skin. And the damned blindfold! "Dale," Jessie said, "do you think you could work your hands around and untie this thing on my eyes? Then I could do yours."

It was a struggle, but, maneuvering and wiggling and positioning themselves just right, they succeeded. Even without the kerchiefs around their eyes, however, they couldn't see a damned thing; it was nearly pitch black inside the box.

"Where do you think we are?" she asked him.

"Can't be too far from Beacon, we didn't ride far enough for that. Sounds like a cow camp—but that couldn't be. Sure are enough of them, though. I'd say seven to ten men, at least, and horses."

"And guns," Jessie added glumly.

"Yeah. Damn fool thing to leave my rifle at the wagon. Could've got us both killed."

"Well, we're lucky to be alive, that's for sure. So quit talking about it. Let's think about getting out of here."

"I've got to fight tomorrow, remember?" Knowlton said.

"You'll be in no shape—if you make it to the ring. They'll have to call it off."

"They'll take a forfeit if I don't show up. Beacon will lose the wager."

It hit Jessie clearly then, and she wondered why she hadn't thought of it two hours ago. "Maybe that's just what they want. Maybe that's why you're here."

"You think it's Goodpaster and his carnival boys? God, I thought you and Ki had killed enough of them to warn them away."

"These men could be newly hired, or his reserves. And no doubt they'll lead Goodpaster right to the farm—and the oil. And it'll all be his, if somebody doesn't show up in that ring and whip Heany."

"I had looked forward to mashing his goddamned brains, what's left of them. They're not going to keep me from enjoying that. I'll get there if I have to crawl."

Jessie stifled a laugh. "We may both be crawling before this is over."

"I can't see that it's funny," he said.

"Oh, Dale." Jessie slid closer to him. She kissed him full on the mouth. Both of them needed it. "If I don't try to smile, I might cry."

She remembered that as a girl she had rarely been afraid—knowing, perhaps, that her father would always be there. Once, when she had gotten lost while out riding, she'd cried and felt alone for the first time in her life. That time ended in the strong, warm grip of her father's arms when he and his men found her. He had been angry with her, and she knew it, but a harsh word wasn't in him. She wished that every time she got in trouble like this, Alex Starbuck would be there to rescue her. But—the sad, icy truth was inescapable—Alex Starbuck was dead; never again would she know the comfort of his embrace.

The two prisoners attempted to work free of the ropes, but it was useless. Even when they lay back to back and tried to untie the knots for each other, they failed. The struggle exhausted them. They could sense that the sun was going down; their box became slightly cooler, the air less stale. The men in the camp went about their business with a minimum of talk and noise.

At one point the sound of a key in the lock pricked up their ears. The door opened for a split second and someone placed a bucket of water on the floor between them. A brief glance at the outside world showed them that, indeed, it was dusk and that they were in open country. But before they could get a better look, the door slammed shut and the lock was replaced. They greedily attacked the water, straining to lift their heads over the edge of the bucket.

"I wonder if they plan to feed us," Dale said.

But the hours passed and night fell and there was no food, and no word from their captors.

Back in Beacon, Ki began to wonder where Jessie and Knowlton were. He knew they had gone out earlier, but he didn't know where. He patrolled the town till past sunset. Still no sign. His instinct for danger was aroused, and he did not like the feeling.

With the fight tomorrow, the future of the town hinging on it, Knowlton's absence cut sharply into Ki's mind. Was there an attempt being made to keep the big man out of the ring with Heany? If so, would the town stand for it? He couldn't speak for the citizens of Beacon, but for himself he meant to see that both Jessie and the young blacksmith were around and unhurt in the morning.

Ki had to assume there was foul play and work from there. Who was most likely to want Jessie and Knowlton hurt or out of the way? His first guess was Goodpaster, the carnival owner and scheming businessman with a criminal record a mile long. Too obvious? Maybe, but that never stopped a man if he desperately needed something done to protect his interests. Ki hadn't yet met Julius Goodpaster— who nonetheless seemed to occupy more and more of his attention these days. Tonight would be as good a time as any to pay the man a visit.

On his way to the local livery stable to procure a horse and find out where the carnival people were camped, Ki passed the lone hotel in Beacon, a saloon with four rooms on top, which the proprietor let for modest nightly rates. Outside the hotel, a lone figure huddled. It was a girl. Ki looked closer, for there was something familiar about her. As he approached, she looked up. It was Yvonne Hunter.

"Ki!" she cried, hurling herself into his arms.

Which of the gods, he wondered, was responsible for this? He held her as she clung to him, sobbing. He stroked her velvet-smooth hair. "Why did you come here?" he asked. "Are you alone?"

Yvonne explained. "I had to follow you—and Miss Jessie. I wanted to be here with you, in case anything happened." She told Ki how she had ridden, alone, all the way from Gilead.

Leaving a note for Mrs. Oxbridge explaining where she was going, Yvonne had set out for Beacon in the early morning, a day behind Jessie and Ki. She wanted to stay well out of their way until she reached Beacon, so that if they discovered her, they could not send her back. Knowing that she'd most likely anger them by this action, Yvonne hoped it would be too late for them to do anything about her presence there. And there was something inside her that compelled her to go.

She had had a dream the night before in which she saw Ki in danger. He had faced danger many times before; but now, since he had come into her life, Yvonne wanted to be there to help him in any way she could. It wasn't anything she could put into words; she just had to go.

The livery man in Gilead had five dollars of hers that had taken her months to save, and she had extracted a promise of silence from him. That would delay any effort by Mrs. Oxbridge to follow her. So she had set out on the hard ride to Beacon. She was scared, she was inexperienced, but she persevered. Now she stood next to her man, ready to help him if she could.

"I had to come," she emphasized through her tears of relief, "to be with you."

Ki felt a strange mixture of pity and pride for this girl. "You could have been hurt—even killed."

"I know," she said, chastised but happy to be in his arms.

"When did you get in?"

"Just a couple of hours ago."

"Did you encounter anyone on the trail?"

"No, not a soul." She could see, in the harsh yellow light from the saloon, that his face was lined with worry. "What's wrong?" Then she sensed it. "Is it Jessie?" She asked. "Has something happened?"

Ki said, "I don't know—yet. She didn't return from a trip outside of town with her friend Knowlton. I fear she is in trouble, along with him." He had to explain to Yvonne who Knowlton was. "He is to fight tomorrow for the town. He's the only man they have to put up against the fighter Heany."

"The one we saw at the carnival in Gilead?"

"Yes, the man with the evil face. I do not like that man."

"The fight is probably crooked anyway," the girl said.

"Probably, but it must be fought if the town is to survive. And Jessie feels that Beacon must survive."

"Does this have anything to do with Mr. Kelso's killing?" Yvonne wondered, beginning to see the connection, yet not fully understanding what was happening.

"Yes," Ki replied simply. "Though we do not understand exactly how or why."

"First," said Yvonne decisively, "we've got to find Jessie."

"First," Ki said with a half-smile, "we must find you a place to stay for the night."

"I'm staying with you."

Ki was ready to force her, if necessary, to stay at the hotel—until he took one look inside of the fleabitten shack with its smell of sweat and piss, warm beer and stale tobacco reeking everywhere. It turned his stomach, and the girl looked ready to cry at the sight and smell of the place. Once outside on the street again, he said, "You will stay with me."

Naturally, that pleased the girl just fine. Ki, on the other hand, now had two women to worry about—Yvonne and Jessie.

He told Yvonne that he planned to pay a call on Julius Goodpaster. She'd have to come along with him—keeping her eyes open and her mouth shut. Goodpaster, he said, might prove to be the key to this whole mess, and he might know Jessie's whereabouts.

"You really care about Jessie, don't you, Ki?"

The samurai confronted her gaze directly. They walked toward the livery. "Yes, Yvonne," he said, "I care for her. More than that, I would die for her if I had to. You see, I serve not only Jessie Starbuck but the memory of her great father, the man who gave me work—and a sense of pride—when I thought I had no chance for either. If it hadn't been for Alex Starbuck, I would probably not be alive now. He gave me life; and I have dedicated that life to him."

"But he's dead," she said. It was a simple statement, from her heart, and she did not mean to be coy or naive.

"To me, he lives on," said Ki. "In Jessie, in her work. And in my heart. Every battle we fight, Jessie and I, we fight for Alex."

"Gee, I hope when I'm dead there'll be somebody left to fight for me."

"There will be, Yvonne. One day you'll be married and become a mother. Your husband and your children will be your armor. They shall protect and preserve your memory."

The girl shivered at all this death talk. "That won't happen for a long time. The husband and babies part of it, that is. At least I hope so. There's too much I want to do yet."

"You've made a good start—riding off like that by yourself. I don't think a husband would allow you to do such a thing."

"Oh, stop it," she said with a playful slap at his arm.

"I'm only telling the truth."

"Well, I don't want to hear it—not right now, anyway."

At the livery they rousted out the sleeping stable boy, who, with a hard look at this strange pair, charged them four bits apiece for two horses. Ki paid up without protest. He and Yvonne were soon saddled up and on their way.

★

Chapter 8

Night found Jessie and Knowlton exhausted and frustrated and thirsty. The water they had been given was gone; their struggle against their bonds had been unsuccessful. It was still hot and stifling in their box, though less so than it had been during the day. The night promised to be a long one.

Jessie held herself against Knowlton, seeking to gain strength from him. She was hungry. She wondered what was going on inside his mind. "What are you thinking, Dale?"

The big blacksmith said, "If only I could get out of these damned ropes, I might be able to force the door."

"Then what? There are men out there, all of them armed. They'd cut you down in a second. I don't want you to try anything foolish, Dale."

"Oh, I've used up all my foolishness for today. I got us in here, didn't I"

"Quit talking like that."

"It's true."

"It isn't, and you know it." Jessie's arms, legs, and back ached from the confining bonds. The rope bit painfully into her wrists, rubbing them raw. "We were both careless, and we're paying for it. But there's got to be a way out."

"When you think of it, be sure to tell me," he said wryly.

"I'll do that," she replied. She turned herself around to face him. In the fetid darkness of their prison she could barely see his face. She kissed him. "We'll make it."

Knowlton was boiling inside. He'd willingly do anything to get Jessie out of this mess. If only he hadn't been so stupid as to leave his rifle at the wagon! But it was too late to change what had already happened. And the fight tomorrow—how the hell would he be able to get out in time to face the killer Heany and repay his old debt to Joshua Johnson? Damn, he thought, it wasn't working out like he'd planned.

"Stop it," Jesse said.

"Stop what?"

"Thinking. I know you, Dale. You're being too hard on yourself. I'm not going to stick around if you keep punishing yourself like that."

"And just where will you go?" he asked, snuggling closer to her, smelling the rich, sweet scent of her hair.

"I'll move to the other side of this box and stay there."

"Okay, then. If it's come to that—I'll stop thinking."

"Good," she said. They kissed passionately, the need rising within them both. If only there were some way to shed these ropes, to make love, to put aside the danger and misery of their predicament.

But reality intruded. They heard someone outside opening the lock. The door swung open and cool, fresh night air swept in. They breathed clean air for the first time in hours.

"Come on," a harsh voice commanded.

It took the captives' eye a few moments to adjust to the light, feeble as it was. Jessie felt a rough hand pulling her toward the door. She found herself dropping to the ground; it was difficult to stand upright after lying in the wagon for so many hours. Knowlton followed her out. She looked at the man who had come for them. He was the tall, dark-skinned man with long black hair—the half-breed who had captured them at the farmhouse. He wore dark pants and beaded moccasins. He carried his Henry repeating rifle, and on his belt he wore a sheathed bowie knife.

As they had guessed, Jessie and Knowlton were in the middle of a camp. Other wagons were scattered about, and several men hunkered around a large fire, drinking coffee and smoking. The half-breed prodded them along with his rifle barrel. Knowlton's face darkened in anger and humiliation. Jessie glanced at him to reassure him, but the blacksmith was sullen, his jaw tense, as he took in everything around them.

The half-breed guided them to a large wagon, set apart from the others. He preceded them up the steps to the door, knocked once, and opened it. "Move," he told them.

Jessie and Knowlton did as they were ordered, making their way up the steps tentatively, trying not to fall over. The tightly tied ropes made any movement difficult and painful. Inside, the wagon was spacious and well appointed. A large man in a white shirt and unknotted silk tie sat at the far end, twirling a glass of brandy in his hand.

"Welcome, Miss Starbuck, Mr. Knowlton," the man said, lifting his glass in salute. The half-breed stood to one side, watching the two prisoners intently. "I am Julius Goodpaster, proud owner of this traveling show."

Jessie and the blacksmith exchanged curious looks. So it was Goodpaster who had kidnapped them. Now it made some sense—though it didn't ease their anger. They didn't say anything.

"I must apologize for making your stay with us so uncomfortable. But, you see, I cannot take any chances."

Jessie listened for a trace of a Scottish accent and heard none. This man was a skilled performer who was very good at covering his tracks. If she hadn't known his background from the information the U.S. marshal's office in Omaha had provided, she couldn't have guessed.

"What do you want with us, Goodpaster?" she said defiantly, holding her head high. She knew she must look ludicrous, trussed up like a calf for branding, but she did not care. She'd show this man that a Starbuck never gave up.

"Steel Knife," Goodpaster said, "please release them. Those ropes make me feel very uncomfortable."

The half-breed unsheathed his gleaming bowie knife. He stepped behind Jessie. She felt the cold steel against her wrists. With a swift upward slash he cut her bonds. The relief was exquisite as she brought her hands around in front of her, rubbing her arms and wrists. She unwound the ropes from her neck and ankles as Steel Knife cut Knowlton's hands free.

"You expect us to thank you?" Knowlton challenged, pulling the ropes away.

"No," said Goodpaster. "I know how unpleasant it is to be confined. I would not take such measures, though, if they were not necessary, you understand."

"I don't understand a bit of it," Jessie blurted. "What are you after, Goodpaster?"

The carnival owner ignored her question. "I've spent time—more time than I care to recall—in prisons of one sort or another. Believe me, I sympathize with you. That may be little comfort—"

"Very little," Knowlton said.

Goodpaster raised his eyebrows and smiled. "Well, I'll give you credit for having sand in your craw, Mr. Knowlton. Looking at you, I can see why the town chose you to accept the challenge I presented to them. You might have given our man Heany a run for his money, at that."

"I mean to whip him bad," Knowlton persisted.

"Well, things don't always work out as one plans, do they?" The carnival owner regarded them smugly. "Please have a seat, the both of you. Care for a drink?"

Jessie shook her head. "Just tell us what you want, Mr. Campbell."

Again, Goodpaster smiled. "You *are* resourceful, Miss Starbuck. I won't ask you how you discovered my sordid past dealings and identity, but I give you the utmost credit. I see now I was dangerously underestimating you. I'll be more careful in the future."

"Your future may be more limited than you think," she challenged boldly.

"Unfortunately, it's not for you to say—neither of you. It's your lives that are at stake here, not mine."

"If that's the case," Jessie said, "maybe you wouldn't mind telling us what this is all about."

"I'm certain you have a good idea, Miss Starbuck. After all, you came all the way to Nebraska from Texas. Your man Kelso, as full of ideas as ever, presented you with some tantalizing information—important information. Important enough, in any case, to bring you here personally."

"How do you know about Kelso's doings?"

"I have my sources of information—very good sources. Are you sure you wouldn't care for a drink?"

"You going to tell the lady what she wants to know?" Knowlton demanded.

"Frankly, no, Mr. Knowlton. I don't believe I'm obliged to do that."

"So why did you bring us here?" said Jessie.

"To offer you a choice, a proposition. I'm not a man who deals unfairly with my enemies."

"Sending bushwhackers to kill us on the trail isn't unfair? Kidnapping Dale and me isn't unfair?" Jessie was seething with anger at this man's overweaning pride and treachery. She didn't buy a word he uttered. "And what about Winslow? Using him to do your dirty work—was that fair?"

"Wallace Winslow is a pig, if you'll pardon my language, Miss Starbuck. He doesn't know what's good for him. He's greedy and dishonest. But he is useful to me. At least he was."

Jessie glanced over at Steel Knife. The half-breed stood there expressionless, taking in everything that was said. She wondered what his relationship with Goodpaster was. Chief enforcer, probably—and a good one. She had to give the crafty carnival owner credit for that.

"What is your proposition?" she said.

"This." Goodpaster rose and went to a cabinet. He brought out her Colt and holster, along with Knowlton's rifle. "These are your weapons. You may take them and leave—and never come back. I will have Steel Knife escort you as far south as the Kansas border. You will promise never to set foot in Nebraska again, and never to interfere with me."

"You're saying the half-breed won't backshoot us the first chance he gets?" Knowlton sneered.

"Steel Knife does what I tell him to do."

Jessie said, "That's not very reassuring."

"You have another choice." The carnival owner lit a cigarette with a sulfur match. "You can hang tomorrow. I've made all the arrangements. The boys have plenty of rope and a lot of time on their hands. It would give them something to do."

Jessie eyed her revolver—a present from her father. She was tempted to make a grab for it right now. But that would be foolish, with Steel Knife standing by, and Goodpaster. She wanted to know more about Goodpaster himself before she killed him. What began as an inkling about him had now grown to a strong suspicion: Was it possible that he was being financed by the cartel? What about the interna-

140

tional connections the telegraph from Omaha had mentioned? She must buy time, take a chance that she and Knowlton could survive long enough to find out. That meant staying here, in Goodpaster's camp, rather than riding out with Steel Knife—who was sure to put a bullet in her back the first chance he got on the open trail.

"We'll stay," she said.

"I thought you would," said Goodpaster. "The boys will be glad to hear it. They've been itching for a necktie party, as they call it."

"What happens to Beacon?" Knowlton asked.

"What was meant to happen. Beacon will lose the wager, unless they can put up a man who can beat Heany. You were their best hope. The prospect of another man doing it, you'll agree, is unlikely."

Knowlton spat on Goodpaster's carpet. Steel Knife stepped toward him and backhanded him hard across the face. The blacksmith bristled, but dared not challenge the tall half-breed. He couldn't take a chance on getting killed and leaving Jessie alone.

A knock on the wagon door broke the growing tension. A man entered and went straight to Goodpaster, whispering in his ear. The carnival owner smiled. "Now isn't that a coincidence." He turned to Jessie and Knowlton. "I'm afraid our discussion is at an end. I have more visitors coming tonight. Steel Knife will escort you back to your quarters. Good night. Or should I say goodbye? We'll not have an opportunity to talk again—in this world, anyhow."

The half-breed prodded them out with his long rifle barrel. From inside the wagon, Goodpaster called out, "Don't bother tying them up again. Let them rest comfortably tonight."

Without another word, Steel Knife took them back and locked them up in the hot, dark little wagon. The lock closed with an ominous click.

• • •

After a long hot day, the cooling night air felt fresh and sharp. And as tired as both Ki and Yvonne were, they felt a jolt of fresh energy as they rode to the edge of Beacon through the dark, deserted streets and out into open country. The livery boy had told them that the carnival was camped about two miles out of town. Ki rode at Yvonne's right hand, ever alert for trouble.

Yvonne's black hair blew back from her face as her mount's pace increased. She took in a deep lungful of the fresh country air and turned her attention to the trail ahead. A strange tingle crept up her spine as the prospect of danger lay ahead, but she was with Ki and she felt safe.

Memories of her night with the gentle Oriental still dominated her thoughts—his tenderness, his passion, the things he had taught her. How different he was from the dull-eyed men and boys of Gilead. In fact, they didn't even qualify as men, compared to the quiet Oriental. She wondered if there was anything between Ki and Jessie Starbuck; he seemed so devoted to her. No, she concluded—Ki would not be unfaithful to Jessie if she were his woman. They were good friends and partners. Still, Yvonne felt somewhat jealous of the fiery-haired young woman who rode with Ki. She couldn't help it. Jessie herself was a breed apart, unlike anyone the girl had ever encountered—an independent, strong, confident woman. And with Ki at her side, there could be no stopping Jessie Starbuck, except perhaps by treachery and dirty-dealing, which Yvonne was determined to help prevent, if she could.

It was a short ride to their destination. As they approached the encampment, Ki counted eight wagons in all, some larger than others, and more than ten men around one central campfire. Although they were well aware of the strangers' presence—he suspected that at least a couple of men stood guard farther out and had probably signaled the approach of the riders—no one moved from the fire as the samurai and the girl rode up.

Reining in, Ki said quietly, "I've come to see Goodpaster."

"That's *Mr.* Goodpaster to you, Chinaman," an anonymous voice spat.

Ki sat his saddle, erect and stonefaced. He repeated his statement, in the same words.

One man, a lanky, long-haired half-breed Indian, rose from the fire and faced Ki and Yvonne. "Mr. Goodpaster know you were coming?"

"No," said Ki.

"In that case, not likely he'll see you."

Ki kept his expression carefully bland as he studied the man who faced him. He noticed the long-bladed knife in the half-breed's belt—near which his left hand dangled easily. Ki guessed that the man was as skilled at throwing it as he was at wielding it in close combat. Ki's own well-used *kodachi* blade was sheathed, and his *katana*, in its lacquered scabbard, hung from the saddle. Neither he nor the half-breed carried a gun. Ki sensed a bizarre kinship with him—as if he faced a brother who served an enemy lord on the field of battle.

"Tell him who I am. He'll see me." Ki slowly, carefully dismounted and directed the girl to do likewise.

"Who might that be?" asked a frog-voiced man sitting at the fire.

"Tell him Ki is here."

The tall half-breed turned and went to the largest wagon in the camp, which was parked nearby. He emerged a short time later with word that Goodpaster would talk to him. He conveyed the message without inflection, simply stating the words, his eyes not leaving Ki for a second. For he too sensed a comrade in arms—a man as dangerous as himself—or potentially so.

Once inside the wagon, Goodpaster regarded both visitors with mild curiosity. "What may I do for you?" he said.

"I'm looking for Miss Jessica Starbuck and the man named Knowlton. If you know where they are, tell me." Ki spoke slowly and evenly, his eyes directly on the carnival owner's.

"You ask the impossible. I don't know where they are. But you better tell that boy Knowlton to show up on time tomorrow to fight Heany—or else this entire town belongs to me by forfeit."

Ki said, "He knows that. And he would not miss the fight by choice. If he is not there tomorrow, it will be because somebody prevented him from showing up."

"And you think I'd be stupid enough to do it?" Goodpaster said in mock astonishment. "You don't know me at all, then, Mr. Ki. I play hard, but I play fair. It's not my way to kidnap or kill people."

"I didn't say anything about killing."

"I know you didn't," Goodpaster countered.

"If Miss Starbuck is dead, I shall kill the man responsible."

"I'm sure you will," Goodpaster said with a smile playing on his lips. "You impress me as a resourceful man. And a loyal one." Goodpaster got a cut-glass decanter from a cabinet. "Care for a brandy, Mr. Ki, Miss—?"

Yvonne introduced herself. Her voice trembled only slightly. She did not like Julius Goodpaster; she saw that he was toying with Ki, and knew that was a dangerous game. The atmosphere inside the wagon was tense, and she wasn't sure what was going on between these two men. Goodpaster's frank, appreciative stare made her uncomfortable.

"A real pleasure, miss," the carnival owner allowed. He was attractive to women, and the fact was not lost on him. He knew how to charm them, to soften them, to take them and throw them away. And always he acted with the utmost politeness, for he realized they liked that too. "Are you a—

a friend of this gentleman? If you're in trouble, I'd be glad to help you out."

"I don't need your help, thank you," said Yvonne. "And yes, I am Ki's friend."

"A good man to have siding you, by the looks of him," Goodpaster went on. He turned to Ki. "Does Miss Starbuck make it worth your while—I mean, does she pay you well enough?"

"Why do you ask?" said the samurai.

"Let's just call it self-interest. You see, I pay well for skilled help. And it's easy to see you're a skilled man, Mr. Ki."

"My skill is not for sale."

Goodpaster shrugged magnanimously, as if to say it meant nothing to him. "Well, if you ever need a job, you might consider hiring on."

"Does this traveling show make enough money to pay for all those hired men we saw outside?" Ki asked.

"Let's just say I have other interests besides the show. Interests that pay substantially."

"And you need many guns for this business."

A sharp edge of anger cut into the carnival owner's voice: "Those men are for protection. They're not skull-busters, if that's what you're implying."

"You Americans place too much value on guns," Ki said, probing Goodpaster to reveal his true identity.

But the man did not betray himself. "Perhaps you place too little. Guns are a way of life out here in the West—a necessary evil. And I don't think they're all that evil. I see you do not carry a gun, Mr. Ki. A dangerous habit."

"No, I choose not to carry a weapon that makes so much noise."

Throughout this exchange, Yvonne prayed silently that Goodpaster did not intend to harm Ki. She thought of all those men outside around the fire—especially the tall, fierce-

145

looking half-breed. Ki was only one man, and they were many. Fear gnawed at her insides, and she wished she were back in Gilead at Mrs. Oxbridge's boardinghouse, helping to serve supper to the boarders. This talk about guns and killing was making her shiver. She edged closer to Ki, wanting him to take her away from here.

Goodpaster returned to his brandy decanter and poured himself a drink from it. "Miss Yvonne, are you sure you don't care to join me in a drink?" He was obviously trying to distract her from Ki's probing questions.

"We're leaving," Ki said. "As long as you can assure me you do not know where Miss Starbuck and Knowlton are."

"I've told you—I have no idea, Mr. Ki. However, I shall alert my men to search the area immediately and to keep their eyes open for Miss Starbuck. I hope she turns up. Maybe she's in Beacon now, looking for you."

"Let's go, Ki," Yvonne whispered.

"I do not think she is," said Ki.

"My men will watch for her—and the man. All I can say is, he'd better show up in that ring. The people of Beacon will be very disappointed if he's not there."

After Ki and Yvonne were gone, Steel Knife came into Goodpaster's wagon. "Do you want me to go after them?" he suggested.

Goodpaster said, "No. As long as we hold Miss Starbuck and the blacksmith, we need not concern ourselves with Mr. Ki and his pretty companion."

Ki and Yvonne stopped about a half-mile outside of Beacon. They had ridden back in frustrated silence. Ki, knowing what he did about Goodpaster, could not believe the man's disclaimers. With his ears cocked for any sign of pursuit, he had kept a steady pace away from the camp. Now it was past midnight as he dismounted. The girl watched him, puzzled.

146

"What are you doing?" she asked him.

"It's time to sleep." He retrieved a blanket he had thought to bring. "I'll prepare a bed for you."

"Out here?" Yvonne stepped down from her horse.

"Better than in town. And I don't want to be anyplace Goodpaster can find us." He laid the blanket out near a tree, folding it double so that she would be able to cover herself. He took the horses and led them a short distance away, tethering them to a sapling. Luckily they had been well fed and watered and hadn't been ridden too hard, so they needed little attention.

When he returned to the blanket, Yvonne was standing there, her hands on her shapely hips. "I'm not going to take the whole blanket. Where are you going to sleep?"

"I'll stand watch for a while."

"What's there to watch for? Ki, I want you to lie down with me. I'm afraid."

"There is nothing to be afraid of," he said.

"I'd feel better if you held me—at least until I fall asleep."

Yvonne opened the blanket and they lay on it together. Ki's arms enveloped her and she fitted the length of her body against his. She sighed and said, "Ki, what do you think has happened to Jessie and that man?"

The samurai said, "I do not know, but I think Goodpaster does. He was lying to us."

"Do you think they might be . . . dead?"

"No. I would know, inside, if she were dead. She is alive, and not far away—of that I am certain."

"Oh, Ki!" Yvonne turned to face him. "What's happening? I don't like it. Something bad is going on, but I don't know what it is—only that you aren't safe. If you get hurt, Ki, I'll die. I will." She buried her head in his chest.

"Don't worry, Yvonne," he said, stroking her hair. "No one will be hurt."

"I couldn't bear it if—if anything happened to you."

Nothing he could say would ease her troubled mind. She

147

clung to him. "Ki, take me away from here—far away. We're alive now. That's all that counts. Please, Ki." She kissed him, her mouth open hungrily.

The night sky had clouded over, obscuring the moon. It was getting colder, but Ki felt a fiery heat growing within him. He kissed her and clutched her tightly to him. Their bodies pressed together tightly and he fought for breath.

"I need to know I'm alive, Ki," the girl said in a husky voice.

The ground beneath them, despite the blanket, was hard; but they did not take much notice. They lay there entwined, her lips against his. Her tongue darted in and out of his mouth. Then her hands were at his chest, her fingers unbuttoning his shirt. She put her hand inside; it felt cold against the warm skin of his chest as she ran her fingers across it.

Ki plunged his hands into her blouse, seeking her breasts. They were firm and full, and he caressed them. Yvonne moaned and gripped his muscular chest, placing her face against his neck, kissing and licking it ravenously. Her tongue burned against his skin and he fondled her nipples a bit more roughly.

"Yes, Ki, do that," she whispered gutturally. His hands massaged her breast and she arched her back.

Then Ki felt one of her hands move to his crotch, groping aginst the tight fabric of his pants. His organ began to stiffen at her touch, and she rubbed frantically there to help it along. She fumbled with the buttons of his fly, finally pulling it open. The girl freed his erection and gave a soft purr to indicate that she had found what she was seeking. His pole was stiff and ready, and she gripped it firmly.

"Are you always ready like this?" she teased him.

"Not always," he said. "You make it happen, girl."

As he talked, his hand traveled from her breasts to her flat stomach. He inched farther down until she stopped him by sitting up. "Let's take off our clothes," she suggested.

Quickly both of them stripped, then lay back down on the blanket.

Ki immediately reached for the furry, musky center of her passion. He gently ran his fingers through the patch of curly hair that guarded her sex, then deftly found the rising nub and rubbed it. The girl bucked and her thighs clamped together, trapping his hand in her crotch. Ki opened her legs again and teased her with his fingers. He traced the swollen lips of the warm, moist region that throbbed so invitingly. Stimulating her rapidly, he felt her shudder with anticipation.

Her eyes met his, and he saw a look of unquenchable need there in the dark depths. Her white, travel-worn face was beautiful and open and branded with desire.

Then Yvonne rose to her knees. Ki helped steady her as she spread her legs wide on either side of his hips. He stroked her dangling breasts and lifted his head to brush the nipples with his lips. The cherry-like nipples hardened in the fresh chill of the air as she positioned herself above him.

Her nether lips met Ki's rising sword, and his legs stiffened. She dropped in a quick plunge, taking all of him inside her. "Oh, God!" she cried. "Ki, it hurts me to have you inside me, but it's a good hurt. You're so hard!"

The girl rocked back and forth on top of him. Above his face, hers rose and fell, her eyes closed tightly. Ki reached down and cradled her buttocks in his hands, helping to lift her and control her rhythm.

"Yes," she sighed as she felt his strong hands there.

Yvonne's pale face was tinged with pink now and her breath came quick and shallow. Their grunts and cries echoed through the night. A thin sheen of sweat covered them both, locked in their love dance.

When she slackened a bit, Ki took charge. He sat up carefully and lifted Yvonne without breaking their connection, then he turned her sideways, laying her down on the blanket facing him. She sighed and adjusted herself, wiggling against the rough blanket and the hard ground. Ki let himself down beside her, his arms locked around her. Slowly at first, he began pumping her.

"Ki, my strong man! That feels so good! Oh, Ki . . ."

She lifted her legs and locked her feet behind his back and pulled him deeper into her. Ki picked up the pace, stroking boldly and quickly. Yvonne held on, her body moving with his, lifting herself to meet his thrusts.

Yvonne brought her lips to his, seeking him for a deep, passionate kiss. Her hands played along his body, from his chest to his ribs, feeling his taut, lean muscles as they flexed and relaxed with his deep strokes. Their rhythm quickened, and they thrust together, the hot core of their spirits in molten union.

"Please do it faster, Ki, please," she asked, her voice high-pitched and urgent.

Ki plunged his engorged length into her harder and faster. This beautiful young woman knew what she wanted, and he would give it to her. He watched her ivory face as she took every inch of him; he pushed himself to the limit to please her and fulfill her.

Yvonne gasped and dug her fingers into his already-bruised arms. Ki wanted to cry out and ask her to let go, but he could not stop to do it. He realized that they were approaching climax and pushed ahead.

Then, suddenly, the girl's body began jerking spasmodically, and he felt the muscles of her love chamber contracting around his shaft. Her soft but strong white legs clamped more tightly around him, demanding that he not cease. So Ki kept on, bringing himself closer to the edge with every long stroke.

She came again and again. Ki felt nothing but hotness and blackness as he plunged roughly in and out of her. Her love juices lubricated his manhood and smoothed its passage. It seemed never-ending and all too brief, then it was over.

With Yvonne's mewing cries in his ears, Ki stopped, buried himself to the hilt, and came. He surprised himself at the force and volume of his climax as he erupted. Rocking back and forth gently, he emptied himself into her.

"I can feel every drop, Ki," she said. "I wish you wouldn't stop loving me."

Ki held her tightly. "Don't ever despair of love, Yvonne," he said. "You will know much love in your life." And he kept holding her until she fell asleep. He dressed her without awakening her and covered her with the blanket.

Before he fell asleep, as he took a brief look around, Ki made a decision. If Dale Knowlton did not show up to fight Heany tomorrow, he'd do it himself.

★

Chapter 9

The canvas ring had been erected in the town square, the rest of the carnival troupe staying outside of town. The low, battered buildings of Beacon offered little shade as the sun climbed higher and hotter in the sky. It was a dry, cloudless day—a fitting day for a fight. The folks of Beacon were out, drifting toward the boxing ring in clusters, some of them eating sandwiches or drinking from whiskey bottles. They were oddly quiet, curious but not afraid. Word had spread that Dale Knowlton was missing and could not fight. They were interested to see who, if anybody, was fighting in his place, though none of the men were interested enough to volunteer to replace Knowlton. The strapping young blacksmith had been their only hope—and a slim one at that.

The carnival fighter, Dennis Heany, was smoking a cheroot on the street beside the ring. He took a swig from a flask he kept in his back pocket. He was talking to Julius Goodpaster, who stood tall and elegantly dressed beside the frayed, dissipated, but still powerful fighter.

Yvonne followed Ki as he made his way through the crowd toward the ring. She looked frantically about, clinging to the hopeless idea of seeing Jessie and Knowlton. "Ki," she said. "Let's wait to see if they turn up."

"There is no more waiting. The town will forfeit the fight if no man steps into the ring. There's no use cursing my *karma*—this was somehow meant to be."

"I can't believe that!" the girl said. "Why do you care what happens to these people? Look at them. They don't give a damn themselves."

Ki did not answer her. It was a question without an answer. As with most difficult situations he had faced, he accepted this fight as a fact, something to be faced and dealt with. Ki had had enough fighting in the past few days to last him a lifetime—in Gilead, on the trail, and here in Beacon. Trouble had stalked him relentlessly all the way. What he didn't need was this boxing match with an old, skilled professional fighter who could beat men twice his size, like Frank Orwell, back in Gilead. Ki was tired and sore and worried about Jessie. His injured arm ached and his mind was equally pained. Once this fight was over— win or lose—he must find Jessie and the big blacksmith. He did not allow himself to think they might be dead.

"Don't worry, girl," he said to Yvonne. He saw tears in her bright, dark eyes.

She stayed behind as Ki went over to Heany and Goodpaster. The immaculately groomed Goodpaster looked Ki over from head to foot, just as he had the previous night, at their first meeting. "I hadn't heard that you are an accomplished fighter—in the ring, that is. You are a man of many talents, Mr. Ki. I'd still prefer to have you on my side."

"From whom do you hear anything about me?" Ki asked pointedly.

Goodpaster smiled, revealing a row of even white teeth. "From my sources. You see, like you, I am a man who does not tell more than he knows."

"Do you know where Miss Starbuck and Dale Knowlton are?"

"You asked me the same question last night. I have no different answer for you today." He said the words flatly, without emotion. Ki felt in his gut that the man was lying.

"I shall find out where they are, and if you had anything to do with their disappearance, you will hear from me."

"I don't take well to threats."

"I'm not threatening, Goodpaster. I am merely stating a fact."

"You'll have to get past this man first," Goodpaster said, turning to Heany. "Put away the whiskey, for God's sake, Heany. You've got work to do."

"Right, boss," the Irishman said, taking at last gulp of the precious liquor. He wiped his jagged mouth with his hand.

Ki said, "The wager stands. If I win the fight, the town gets its money. Are you prepared to pay, Mr. Goodpaster?"

"Oh, I'm prepared to pay. But I don't expect to. Do I, Heany?"

"Huh?" The pugilist was startled at being addressed. "Sure, boss," he muttered.

Even if the Irishman was half-drunk, Ki knew better than to let down his guard. Heany had fought so many times— probably more times drunk than sober—that he could probably do it in his sleep.

Heany climbed into the ring and started limbering up, throwing punches at an imaginary foe. Ki followed him onto the canvas, from which the sun reflected glaringly. He looked around at the faces of the people of Beacon. In them he did not see the remotest compassion or concern. He wondered what was going on in their minds. Were they even on his side? Perhaps they had given up long ago, as Yvonne insisted. The samurai located Ettinger at the fringe of the spectators. The attorney was snaking through the people on his way to the ring, nursing a bottle of whiskey along the way.

Ki pulled his loose white shirt off and tossed it to Yvonne, outside the ring. His bronzed chest was lean but muscular, tapering to a thin waist and flat stomach. He wore his usual denims, and was barefoot. His long black hair fell nearly to his shoulders. Puzzled, concerned as to the whereabouts of Jessie and Knowlton, he'd have to do his best against this tough pugilist. Not only did he have a weight disadvantage against Heany, but Ki did not know the rules of boxing that governed this match. Not that Heany would stick to the rules; Ki would be on the lookout for that.

In his corner, Dennis Heany squatted and flexed his muscles. Julius Goodpaster whispered something to the fighter. Heany nodded and smiled, showing the fragmentary teeth still attached to his gums. Also shirtless, the boxer wore tight-fitting brown pants, and high black boots securely laced. Not a very tall man, he was nonetheless quite bulky and heavily muscled. His arms were long and powerful looking, with well-developed biceps; his forearms were like tree trunks. The scowl on his battered Irish mug did nothing to enhance his appearance; in fact, his mouth was like a twisted scar that would never fully heal.

The same short, plump, pinstripe-suited man who had presided at the fight back in Gilead came into the ring and announced the great event in loud and flowery language. Meanwhile, Ettinger had made it through the crowd and scrambled into the ring.

The townspeople watched, listened, waited for the fight to start. They whispered among themselves about Knowlton—where the hell was the man? They didn't know this slim Oriental man who moved with the grace of a cat, but they'd get a fight out of him. Bottles passed back and forth among the men, and the women chatted among themselves about how shameful men were. Lost to the townspeople was any thought that Ki—and they themselves—might lose everything they had; they were all caught up in the excitement of the moment.

Ki felt differently. As the barker wound up his spiel and Ettinger removed his coat, the samurai summoned up all the inner strength he had, and calmness swept over him like a cool breeze. He would fight this man as best he knew how; he would try to win for the town the self-respect it had sloughed off like a snakeskin. Ultimately, though, he was not doing if for these people; he was doing it for himself and for Jessie. As a man of pride he could do no less.

Glancing over his shoulder to locate Yvonne, he saw an unwelcome face pressing close to the ring—Wallace Winslow. Had he come all the way from Gilead just to see the fight? Unlikely, Ki thought. But just then the bell rang to start the first round.

Remembering how the kid in Gilead was beaten by standing still, Ki turned away from Winslow and moved cautiously out to the center of the ring. Heany was there before him, his feet wide apart, his knotted fists raised in challenge. The fighters' faces glistened in the hot sun as they circled each other. Ettinger stayed well clear of them both.

Heany weaved closer—close enough for Ki to smell the whiskey and sweat of his opponent. With an evil grin on his weathered face, Heany said, "You're gonna live to regret this, Chinaman. I can promise you that."

Ki did not respond. He moved from side to side, Heany following him. Suddenly, Heany launched a straight-armed right that caught Ki by surprise, clipping him in the side of the head, rocking him back. Heany followed with another quick right jab that stunned Ki again. He recovered in time to block the third right.

157

This flurry brought the assembled townsfolk to life. There were catcalls, and a few women fainted. Heany glanced over the ropes at them, grinning. Ki saw his opportunity; he unloaded a left at Heany's head, catching him on the cheek.

Heany wheeled around and charged Ki, delivering a flurry of blows at body and head. Ki brought his arms in to shield himself from the attack, absorbing punishment in his body to save his face. Heany, his small dark eyes glinting, closed in and loosed a vicious right hook that narrowly missed as Ki leaped back to avoid it. The samurai darted along the ropes, just out of Heany's reach, as he tried to recover his balance and shake off the pain. Already his recently injured arm was throbbing.

The pugilist wiped his face, which was awash in sweat. He tracked Ki, who feinted right and left, moving on the balls of his feet. Ki watched him, figuring that there was little he could do at this point to overcome the man's raw power; the only thing to do was let him wear himself down and avoid a killing blow early. It was not going to be easy; he'd have to fight intelligently and be patient, and keep the fight alive for several more rounds at least.

Heany, on the other hand, had no such plan. All he wanted was to beat the shit out of Ki, to win the wager and collect his pay from Goodpaster and get back to his bottle. He was confident of his own power and skill; he just needed that one clear shot to the chin to finish this yellow scum. And he'd get it, he told himself. The Chinaman, it was already apparent, knew nothing about boxing.

The first round ended with a loud clatter of the triangle dinner bell suspended from its two-by-four supports. The pinstriped man was keeping time. Ki went to his corner. Yvonne threw him a cloth to wipe his face and body. Her eyes were pleading with him to stop, but she knew better than to say anything. Ki was the kind of man who never quit, once he had begun a task. Nor would he be ruled by the tears of a woman—ever. She whispered a prayer as he moved into the ring for the second round.

"You all right, Mr. Ki?" Ettinger asked him as the bell clanged. "I don't want to see you get hurt."

"Shut your face, mister," Heany growled, "or you'll be the hurt one."

The referee, realizing that his role in the fight was just for show, moved apart from the two fighters. He too knew little of the Marquis of Queensberry rules, but he was determined to see that Ki did not get killed.

Ducking and weaving, Ki avoided Heany's right jabs. He began to be aware that Heany depended almost solely on his right. The Irishman peppered the air around Ki's head with his fists. Planting his feet wide apart, Heany tried a left uppercut. Ki moved just in time to block it, driving the arm down and punching the man in the belly, hard. Heany grunted and swung his free right fist around, landing it in Ki's midsection. Ki felt the air rush from his lungs and struggled for breath. He took a left to the chest and a right to the jaw that sent him backpedaling into the ropes. His arms windmilling as he tried to grab hold of something, anything, he landed on his back on the canvas.

The crowd roared in his ears, and Ettinger stepped between the fighters. Ki tried to suck in some air. He looked up in time to see Heany standing there, laughing at him. Ettinger held Heany back. Ki rolled over and pushed himself to his feet. The people of Beacon cheered him, but he paid them no attention. As he caught his breath and regained his equilibrium, Ki waved the referee away. Heany moved in, grinning evilly. Ki worked his bruised jaw; it would hurt like hell the next day—if he lived that long. He gathered all his powers of concentration to face the plug-ugly pugilist.

Heany circled again, his muscled arms raised theatrically. He and Ki traded blows, their fists glancing off each other. Worn as he was, Ki summoned up all the strength and patience he possessed; he must not let Heany set the pace—

that could be a fatal mistake. Ever alert to his opponent's movements, he ducked as Heany advanced, swinging. Ki came up punching, landing mean blows in the man's belly, chest, and neck. Heany wheeled away, then stepped in again. He returned Ki's surprising attack, launching a combination of rights and lefts, one of which caught the samurai in the kidney, sending a screeching pain throughout his body.

Right, left, right, left. Ki tried to ward off the blows with his arms. Heany then tried to reverse the combination, but in doing so, he confused himself. Ki took advantage of the momentary lapse to drive home a fist to the face. The bell rang just as Heany howled like an injured bear. Ki ducked under the boxer and retreated to his corner.

There he caught sight of Winslow again. The burly hotel owner had made his way over to Goodpaster. The two of them were locked in conversation. No telling what they were talking about—but it most surely added up to no good, whatever it was.

Throughout the third round, Heany tasted his own blood. It dripped from his nose as a result of Ki's surprise attack. Ki wisely stayed out of Heany's way, blocking punches and staying just out of range—not even hoping for a chance to get inside on the Irishmen. This strategy frustrated Heany, making him work harder. But he didn't get any results, and the round ended before he could land a decent punch. In the fourth, Ki pursued the same course, but Heany had had enough; he meant to take charge of the fight and finish it.

The Irishman charged into Ki, his arms swinging, his oak-hard fists hammering away. Ki jerked this way and that, blocking the punches with his weary arms. Heany let his professional instincts take over, finding holes in Ki's defense, battering his opponent's body with all his strength—which was plenty. Ki took the punishment without giving ground, but without giving any back, either. They were close in, now, fighting head to head, trading flurries. But

Heany was unable to deliver the knockout blow that would end the battle.

Keeping his wits as best he could, Ki again noticed that Heany's left was much weaker than his powerful right. So he began to concentrate his attack—what there was of it—on the pugilist's left side, taking punches there while blocking the man's right fist. He hit at the side and belly, working his way up until he found a wide opening and loosed a smart, vicious right to Heany's exposed neck, right below the ear.

Heany's head snapped back and he howled. Blood flew from his injured face. Ki stepped back to catch his breath. The gallery of townspeople was rumbling now, surprised that the Oriental had lasted this long and inflicted this much damage on the professional. Goodpaster shot a troubled scowl at his man. Heany, though, was not intimidated in the least.

"You son of a bitch," he hissed through the blood that dripped from his nose into his mouth. He spat red and came on again. He might very well have beaten Ki to a pulp right there and then, but the round ended just in time.

In his corner, Ki labored for breath. Yvonne ladled water to his lips from a bucket she had fetched for him. "Ki, don't go on with this. To hell with them," she urged him. "It's not worth your getting killed."

Ki shook his head. "I must finish this."

Ettinger checked with both men to discover whether either of them had had enough. Ki gave him the same answer.

The following three rounds were like a bloody eternity for both men. The crowd swayed between dead silence and bursts of cheering for the Oriental defender of their town. No one had expected the match to go on for so long. Silent and unperturbed in Heany's corner, Goodpaster smoked one of his expensive cigarettes. Winslow, too, watched impassively.

By the eighth round, Ki and Heany moved unsteadily

161

around the ring. Heany suddenly regained the offensive. If he had lost strength, it wasn't apparent now. He hit Ki with streaking blows, right and left, which were impossible to guard against. This time Ki was pushed back under the rain of fists. Then he saw Heany's deadly right coming at his face. A white and yellow light flashed in his head as Heany landed a hamlike fist just below his left eye, closing it. Heany followed up with a series of blows to the face and chest.

Ki swung wildly, in shock and pain. The left eye would not open, so he gave up on it, fighting back as well as he could with impaired vision. For the first time in the fight, he was angry; his self-control was slipping away.

He countered with all he had, but was driven back yet again, Heany taking charge with his masterful right hand, poking through Ki's arms and using his own left to defend himself. Ki swallowed his pride and anger, knowing they would get him nowhere. He moved in closer to Heany to diminish the effectiveness of his opponent's fists. Soon they were trading inside blows, one for one. Ki drove his left into Heany's gut, following with a hard right. That took Heany back a step. With only one good eye, Ki had to be careful, but he mustn't completely forfeit the offensive to Heany.

The professional boxer's face was contorted, the fleshy, crimson pulp that was his battered nose giving him a sinister aspect. Ki punched at the face with an uppercut that closed Heany's mouth, then a direct left at the nose. Heany screamed, the pain too much for him to take. Like an angry, giant bear he clawed at Ki, but Ki fended off the blows, punching with precision. He wanted to end this thing before he ran out of energy, before his arms were too heavy to lift. He could only hope that Heany weakened before he did, but there was little sign of that.

The townspeople were screaming now. Ki heard them chant, "Finish him! Finish him!" The bloodthirsty cry rose as if in one voice. But, far from being able to finish off the Irishman, Ki was barely holding his own, remaining erect on his bare feet.

They staggered through the ninth and tenth rounds, hurting and exhausting each other. But neither man was ready to quit. They were no longer fighting to win the wager; they were battling each other out of pure killer instinct.

In the eleventh round, seemingly inspired by Goodpaster's urgings in his corner, Heany came out renewed, ready to fight again. Ki, the left side of his face sore and swollen, his eye closed, his wounded arm almost useless, his body racked with pain from head to toe, got ready for more. His entire frame was shaking, his heart racing, his lungs pumping desperately for air. He felt hot and cold all at once, and with only one good eye—and that one misted over with sweat—he could barely see the powerful, long-armed Irishman coming at him. But he felt Heany's hot breath and smelled the whiskey-and-sweat stink of his body as he approached. And again the two men were locked in close combat, trading punches to the body, punishing each other beyond endurance.

Ettinger had long ago given up any idea of regulating the fight. He circled around Ki and Heany and would intervene only if one man was clearly killing the other.

Ki stepped back and swung his left fist in a roundhouse punch that missed Heany's head. The boxer grinned devilishly as he quickly leaped into the gap and cracked Ki's jaw soundly with that still-effective right. Ki staggered but straightened up. His head spinning, he summoned all the power he possessed to stand and fight. His knees felt like sand and his mouth was on fire. Again, anger crept into his mind—anger at Heany and at Goodpaster and at Winslow, but mostly at the cowardly townsfolk. No one would be too unhappy if he was beaten, despite their ghoulish cheering. He vowed, however, not to give them the satisfaction of seeing him go down for their sake. And Jessie's image kept creeping into his mind; he couldn't stop worrying about her, wherever she was. For her too, he would fight on.

Back at Goodpaster's camp, Jessie and Knowlton waited all morning for the promised hanging party. Through the night, Knowlton had tried his strength on the door, but to no avail. They were trapped in their prison wagon. As the sun rose higher in the sky, they heard the men in the camp getting rowdy. It sounded as if they were drinking.

"They're having quite a celebration out there," Jessie said.

"I won't let them hang you, Jessie," the blacksmith declared. "I don't care about myself—but they won't get you."

"That's funny, I was going to say the same thing to you."

"Don't joke like that. Goodpaster means business."

"The one I'm worried about is Steel Knife, the halfbreed. He's more dangerous than all the other men combined. If we can get past him—"

"There are still the others, a lot of them. We're in a bad way, Jessie."

"It should be over, one way or another, pretty soon." She too was worried, for on the face of it they didn't have a ghost of a chance. Something inside her, though, would not give up. As long as she was alive, she would do whatever it took to keep on living.

The sound of someone fumbling with the lock brought them to attention. Jessie reached for Dale and kissed him. "If we can get hold of a gun," she whispered, "and head for Goodpaster's wagon—we might have a chance."

"Stick close to me," he said. "Don't let them separate us."

The door swung open and a grinning man with several days' worth of whiskers stood there. "C'mon out and join the party," he said. His voice was slurred and his eyes were unfocused. He carried a Greener shotgun under his right arm and held a half-empty whiskey bottle in that hand, while a key ring dangled in his other hand.

Jessie looked at Knowlton and nodded. This was their best and maybe their only chance. In one lunging movement, Knowlton was up and out of the wagon, tackling the man to the ground. Jessie followed him out. As the man fell, he dropped the big scattergun. Knowlton cracked him in the face with his fist and rendered him unconscious. Jessie picked up the gun and looked around. The men in camp were milling around the smoking campfire, shouting and laughing among themselves. Jessie and Knowlton had only a few seconds.

"Dale, see if he has extra shells on him," she said.

Knowlton found several shells in the downed man's pockets. He dropped them into Jessie's vest pocket.

They hugged the far side of the wagon, away from the carnival men at the fire. Goodpaster's wagon lay some forty yards from where they stood, with a few wagons along the way that they could use for cover.

"Did you see the half-breed?" Jessie asked Dale.

"No sign of him—at least not with the other men."

"That's lucky, anyway—unless he's hiding out somewhere."

"We'll have to take that chance."

Jessie agreed. She and Knowlton began their progress toward Goodpaster's wagon. As they ran from the prison wagon to the cover of another one nearby, a shout rose from the men at the campfire. They edged up to the end of the wagon and watched as the men rushed toward the man Knowlton had struck. In the brief moment of confusion, Jessie and Knowlton managed to run another twenty yards, across mostly open space.

Then, as they approached Goodpaster's wagon, one of the carnival men stepped into view with his rifle leveled at them. Reflexively, Jessie raised the double-barreled Greener and squeezed the trigger. The man fired simultaneously, but his bullet went wide. The powerful scattershot from Jessie's gun tore into the man, shredding him from head to gut and washing away his face in a spray of blood and bone. Jessie and Knowlton ran on.

Now they heard the men behind them, alerted to their position by the shotgun explosion. Hot lead snapped through the air around them. They dodged behind the nearest wagon, still ten yards short of Goodpaster's. Jessie reloaded the Greener and handed it to Knowlton.

"Take this." She handed over the spare shells. "Keep me covered as best you can. I'm going on to the wagon to get our guns."

Before he could protest, she was off, streaking across open ground. Knowlton loosed a single blast at the carnival man closest to him. It took the man in the leg and stopped him cold. The others scattered for cover, but they kept firing.

Jessie bounded to Goodpaster's wagon. She got to the door and pushed. It was locked! She cursed wildly under her breath, and looked around. At the base of the short stairway she saw a brick that was used as a support. She leaped to the ground and dislodged the brick. The stairway itself tilted crazily, hanging half-suspended in the air. Gingerly she made her way back to the door and pounded with all her strength at the lock. She heard shots behind her. One bullet slammed into the wagon just a few feet from her head. She hit at the door again and again with the brick until finally it splintered and swung open.

She went directly to the cabinet where Goodpaster had stored their weapons. She found them inside, still loaded, thank God. Quickly, Jessie strapped on her gunbelt. Glancing around the wagon as the battle outside continued to rage, she looked for any other weapons to take. There were none. Then her eyes landed on Goodpaster's desktop. Without bothering to examine them more closely, she swept up the papers and letters that lay there. She folded them quickly and stuffed them into her back pockets. Then she was out the door.

Firing as she ran, Jessie rejoined Knowlton, who was barely holding his own. Her arrival allowed him to reload the scattergun—which was fairly inaccurate at this range. She kept the men at bay with well-placed shots at their positions. Taking more careful aim at one of the men, she was able to wing him, reducing their number by another man.

"We've got to get the hell out of here," Dale breathed as he moved to the opposite side of the wagon and fired at one man who was sneaking up on them. The fellow took a dose of lead in his midsection that blew his intestines out his back. Three down and at least a half-dozen to go. Already they were bucking the odds, but if they stuck around much longer, the numbers would catch up with them.

"There are horses over there," Jessie said, pointing to a small rope corral that held several animals. "We'll have to make a break for it."

They were pinned down, however, by the steady barrage of lead from the carnival men. Still no sign of Steel Knife— for which they were grateful. And there seemed to be no single leader among their enemies; they were disorganized, and most of them seemed as drunk as skunks, thanks to their premature celebration. Nonetheless, there were too many of them, and they kept up a steady fire.

One bullet chipped away a chunk of wood at the corner where Jessie stood. The splinter flew into her face, cutting her right cheek. She ignored the pain and jacked another round into the chamber. Raising the rifle to her shoulder, she fired. Her bullet caught one man in the groin, and she saw the flooding crimson stain there before he collapsed.

Knowlton wasn't having much success, but his well-timed blasts kept the men at a distance. "I'm running out of shells," he called to Jessie.

167

"We've got to try for the horses," she replied, squeezing off another shot that barely missed a man darting between two wagons.

Their ranks were thinned somewhat, but the carnival men still presented a strong threat. Jessie and Knowlton would have to trust to Providence to stay with them on this escape.

Emptying another barrel, Knowlton ducked back behind the wagon and came over beside Jessie. "I've only got two more rounds." He loaded the Greener.

Jessie tossed him his rifle. "Take this." She whipped out her Colt revolver and fired three rapid shots. Then she passed a handful of ammunition to Knowlton. He reloaded his rifle. Jessie stepped back and thumbed three rounds from the loops in her gunbelt to replace the bullets in her gun. "It's now or never," she said.

Without another word they bolted away from the cover of the wagon and toward the corral. It took the camp defenders a few seconds to realize what was happening. Then Jessie and Knowlton could feel the hot wind of bullets ripping by them like angry bees. The blacksmith carried both his rifle and the shotgun. Jessie had holstered her revolver and now ran full speed for the horses. She picked a tall brown gelding that looked fast and powerful. Jumping over the rope that encircled the corral, she came up cautiously to the horse, which was neighing in panic as hot lead sprayed the air. She managed to mount the animal without trouble, and stroked its long neck to quiet its fears.

Knowlton gripped both guns in his powerful left hand and leaped onto a gray stallion. He was not a horseman, but had learned enough in the army to know how to calm his mount and direct it away from the oncoming carnival men. The horse whickered and stamped and circled the pen before jumping the rope in one graceful, high-stepping movement.

Jessie's mount followed. The animals snorted and tossed their heads. It was tough to control them without proper halters—the animals were bitted but not saddled. Just as they turned to ride away, one loud shot rang out from close range.

Knowlton felt his stallion absorb a bullet in his flank. The horse jerked to a halt, kicked, and went down, spilling his rider to the ground.

Turning to see what had happened, Jessie brought her mount around. Filling her fist with her Colt, she shot the man responsible, placing the bullet through his neck. She rode around to Knowlton. He was unhurt. He stood and unleashed both barrels of the Greener at the onrushing men. Two fell screaming as buckshot ripped into their upper bodies. The blacksmith then dropped the shotgun and, holding his rifle, jumped onto Jessie's horse. As she kneed the animal forward, Knowlton turned and pumped more lead into the surging advance of men and powdersmoke.

Then they were safely away and riding for Beacon.

★

Chapter 10

Steel Knife stood by Goodpaster and Winslow as the fight dragged on in the hot town square. He had arrived during the thirteenth round, as both Ki and Heany were staggering. The crowd of spectators was subdued; no clear winner was emerging, and it was turning into a grotesque struggle for survival between the two men.

"What if he beats Heany?" Winslow asked Goodpaster in a hushed, anxious tone. He wiped his brow with his handkerchief.

"Shut up," Goodpaster said shortly. He was more than a little angry at this turn of events. He'd have some words with Heany when it was all over. And he wanted Winslow out of his sight—permanently. He'd talk to the half-breed and arrange it. The greedy hotel owner had become too much of a liability, and Goodpaster knew that he'd never be able to trust Winslow again—not after the girl had bested him and discovered his connection with the scheme in Beacon. Yes, he decided, the sooner Winslow was out of the way, the better.

Goodpaster turned to Steel Knife. "I don't know if it was such a good idea for you to leave before the boys finished their job."

"Don't worry, boss," the half-breed said, "I warned them that if they didn't do it right, they'd pay for it. The girl and the man will be swinging by now."

Winslow overheard this and said, "What is he talking about, Goodpaster? What girl and what man?"

"It is not your concern," the carnival owner snorted.

"If you mean the Starbuck girl and Knowlton, you're inviting trouble. You never told me you were going to have them strung up." The color had drained from his face as he realized what the implications of a lynching might be. It could bring down the full force of the law on their heads. He hadn't bargained for this wholesale butchery when he signed on with Goodpaster.

"I told you, it is not your concern. If you had kept her out of the way as planned, none of this would have been necessary. You've failed me, Winslow. You're fortunate that I'm a generous man, or else I would have arranged for you to hang with them."

Winslow was livid. "By God, man, you've gone crazy! This godforsaken little town and its little oil deposit isn't worth all the killing. What harm did Jessie Starbuck ever do you? I'll admit she's a troublesome little bitch, but—"

"*Was* a troublesome bitch," Goodpaster corrected him. "My superiors will be pleased to learn she is out of the way permanently. She has been a thorn in their side for a long time now. That alone will secure my position in their eyes."

It had taken until now, but Winslow was finally aware of how deeply he had committed himself to this bloodthirsty man and his "superiors," a mysterious group of businessmen who were nameless and faceless but wealthy enough and

172

powerful enough to finance this mad takeover of a remote town in Nebraska for its potential petroleum reserves. The hotel owner turned his attention to the fight in the ring.

Ki, fighting with one eye, was holding his own against the strong but waning prizefighter. The pace of the match had slowed as each man showed signs of exhaustion. Ki was in much better physical condition than his opponent, whose drinking and dissipation were evident now that the fight had lasted this long—much longer than he was accustomed to.

Winslow looked across the ring to Ki's corner. There he saw the girl Yvonne. Fear and concern gripped her, he could tell. And he was reminded of the Japanese man's companion, the woman who was dead by now, if Goodpaster could be believed—Jessie Starbuck. Regret washed over Winslow as he looked back on his dealings of the past few days and weeks. In one sense, he knew he wouldn't have acted any differently, no matter what. Still, he had become oddly fond of the fiery-haired young woman, and he wished he could have persuaded her to throw in with him against Goodpaster, thus preventing even more useless killing. He knew who had killed Kelso, on Goodpaster's orders, and was sick at the thought—and at his own complicity in the crime.

He retraced every sordid step along the way that had brought him here to Beacon at Goodpaster's side. The man was mad—power-mad and money-mad. Now he had killed the Starbuck girl and the blacksmith who was supposed to face Heany. It was too much for Winslow to take, yet he had to keep his mouth shut or risk death himself.

The sun slanted down on the ring, bathing the fighters in heat and sweat and misery. They fought on. Even Ettinger, the hapless referee, was moving with difficulty, trying to keep the match fair—as much as he possibly could. The whole affair took on a dreamlike quality, the shimmering heat-haze slowing the fighters' movements and dazzling the eyes of the dulled spectators. The thirteenth round ended with the hollow clang of the triangle, and the two men retreated to their corners, breathing heavily.

Ki's face was bloodied and swollen, his good eye blackened and sore. If only he could use his *te* fighting skills, he could finish Heany off in a minute. But they were bound to fight by Marquis of Queensberry rules, which limited the fighter's options. At the sound of the bell for the fourteenth round, he dragged himself to the center of the ring. Heany, looking like a monster with a man's body—his face, too, reduced to bloody pulp—raised his fists and beckoned Ki to advance.

"Let's finish this," he whispered harshly, barely able to speak through his twisted mouth. "C'mon, Chinaman."

As Ki stepped forward, he heard the sound of a horse's hooves pounding through the nearby streets. He ducked under a roundhouse blow and moved to the side of the ring. There he saw the horse, a tall brown gelding, galloping for the town square. And riding the animal—he squinted his good eye to be sure—were Jessie Starbuck and Dale Knowlton.

Heany planted a fist in Ki's kidney, doubling the samurai over in pain. Ettinger moved in to pull the fighter away, but Heany kept pummeling Ki.

At the approach of the riders, the crowd buzzed with interest. What was happening? Then someone recognized Knowlton. "Thar's Dale! It's him! Knowlton! Look, it's him!" The people surged toward the approaching horse.

Winslow looked at Goodpaster. The carnival owner stared in disbelief at the sight of the two riders. "How the hell—?" he muttered. Then he turned to Steel Knife. "Get our horses, quick." The half-breed dashed off, weaving his way through the crowd.

"They got away," Winslow exclaimed—half in horror, half in relief. "They didn't hang."

"Damn them, they'll die for this," Goodpaster declared. Reaching inside his coat, he drew a hideout pistol, a Smith

174

& Wesson .32 with a short barrel. "Out of my way!" he roared at the townspeople. Before he could take a step closer to his intended targets, he felt a pair of hands holding him back. He looked around; it was Winslow.

"This has got to stop, Goodpaster. I can't let you do it. There's been enough killing."

"Not nearly enough," Goodpaster hissed. "Let go of me or you'll take a bullet where it hurts."

"Listen to reason, man. It's over and done with. They've escaped. Let's get out of here."

"That bitch has to die, and her boyfriend too," the carnival owner insisted, a killing light in his eyes as he struggled to free himself from Winslow's strong grip. "Let go, I say!"

"I won't let you. Listen to reason, Good—"

Winslow was cut short as Goodpaster turned and planted the .32 in his stomach. He pulled the trigger. The roar was muffled as the barrel pushed against the big man's fleshy midsection. Winslow's eyes went wide with pain and shock as the bullet ripped through his organs. Goodpaster pulled the pistol away. Blood spilled out of the gaping wound, staining Winslow's white shirt. The burly hotel owner stood stock-still, his life flowing out of him. Then, suddenly, he crumpled to his knees and fell facedown in the street.

A woman screamed. Goodpaster looked around in panic. Where was Steel Knife, where were the horses? He saw Jessie and Knowlton ride up to the ring. They looked around at the sound of the shot and saw Goodpaster. He lifted the small pistol and fired three times, missing them, but sending them off their horse.

Steel Knife rode through the crowd, pulling another horse behind him. Goodpaster pushed the people out of his way and ran to the horse and leaped into the saddle. He spent his remaining bullets in the air to warn the crowd off, and he and Steel Knife wheeled and rode away.

Jessie pushed to the fringe of the crowd and raised her

175

revolver, triggering a shot at the fleeing carnival owner. She missed and fired again. This time she thought she might have hit Goodpaster, but he rode on. He and Steel Knife disappeared in a cloud of dust. They were headed back to the camp. She turned her attention to the boxing ring.

Knowlton had jumped into the ring as Heany was viciously punishing Ki. The samurai could not defend himself adequately any longer, and Ettinger wasn't able to pull them apart. The big blacksmith, however, moved in and took charge, pushing Ettinger away. He grabbed Heany by the neck and yanked him off Ki. The pugilist turned to face Knowlton.

Ettinger helped Ki out of the ring and into Yvonne's arms as the two new antagonists squared off. Heany cried out, "This ain't fair!"

Stripping off his shirt and tossing it aside, Knowlton said, "No, it ain't. But I aim to put you under, Heany—like it or not." He launched a left jab that caught the Irishman at the tip of his chin, sending him staggering back against the ropes.

"You got no call—" Heany whined. He lifted his arms to block another punch. He was angry, confused, already hurting from his long bout with Ki. His head spun in agony.

Knowlton moved in. "I got plenty of call, mister. I'm going to cripple you good. You'll never fight again."

"Why?" the desperate boxer asked as he took the bigger man's punches.

"You killed a friend of mine a long time ago. Now you pay."

Heany moved along the ropes, trying to avoid the onrushing Knowlton. He struggled to regain his breath. Then, sensing the younger man's seriousness of purpose, he gathered what was left and lashed out, using his left hand to hold Knowlton at bay. But the blows had no effect on the angry blacksmith. Knowlton kept coming. He stung Heany with a mean uppercut that shut the Irishman's mouth and broke some teeth. Then he unleashed a series of gut punches that drove the air out of Heany's lungs and sent him retching over the side of the ring. The blacksmith stepped back to observe his handiwork. Heany was suffering badly, and there was more to come as long as he stayed on his feet.

Meanwhile, Jessie heard someone call, "A wounded man! He's real bad hurt!" She rushed over to find Winslow barely clinging to life, his insides destroyed by a single bullet at point-blank range. She helped a man turn him over and called for water. The crowd of curious onlookers pressed around them tightly and she ordered them away. "Give us some air," she told them.

She propped Winslow's head up on her lap. He opened his eyes, dark circles of pain and death. He recognized her. "Miss... Starbuck..."

"Don't try to talk," she said. "Is there a doctor around?" she asked. A man went to fetch the local sawbones. She wondered what the hell Winslow was doing in Beacon.

He seemed to understand her unspoken question. "Came to town... to see... Goodpaster. He's... mad... crazy with killing. Glad to see... you didn't hang."

"I hate to say it, Winslow, but it was no thanks to you. Who shot you?"

"Goodpaster... son of a... bitch. I told him... had to stop... but he... wouldn't listen... mad, I tell you. God, it hurts!"

"Lie still," she told him. She tore his shirt off and saw the bullet hole. It was a ghastly wound, and she could barely look at it. She wadded the shirt and pressed it against the hole, trying to stanch the flow of blood, but it was no use. He was as good as dead.

"Must tell you... sorry... didn't want you hurt." It was difficult to hear him; his breath was shallow, his face pasty and lifeless.

"Why did you do it, Winslow? Couldn't you see Goodpaster was no good? He's a killer."

"He killed Kelso...had the 'breed do it. I knew then...insane."

Jessie wasn't surprised. It made sense. Goodpaster had moved in, enlisted Winslow, and killed Kelso. But how had he found out about the Beacon discovery in the first place?

Winslow struggled to speak. "Worked for somebody...businessmen...never told me...who..."

She leaned down and held her ear to his mouth to catch his words. But there were no more words. Winslow expelled his last breath and died. A man arrived with a pitcher of water, but it was too late. She laid his head down in the dust.

As Jessie stood, she saw Knowlton in the boxing ring, giving Heany the beating of his life. Mercilessly the big blacksmith pummeled the man. Heany reeled around the ring and Knowlton pursued him. Finally, with a smashing right, Knowlton lifted the Irishman off his feet and sent him crashing to the canvas.

It took several hours for the furor of the afternoon to subside and the people of Beacon to return to their homes. By nightfall it was all over, the canvas ring dismantled and the townsfolk dispersed. Jessie and Knowlton had taken Ki to the blacksmith's room behind his shop. Jessie was surprised to see Yvonne, but grateful that the girl was there to help out—and she extracted the story of the girl's bold ride from Gilead.

"I'll take care of Ki," Yvonne promised Jessie. The samurai lay sleeping on Knowlton's bed, his cuts washed and bandaged. It would be a day or more before he could travel back to Gilead and, from there, home to Texas.

Jessie, however, faced one more item of unfinished business—she had to find Julius Goodpaster. Outside, in his blacksmith shop, she found Knowlton. She told him she must ride out in the morning to track the killer.

"Get some rest first, girl," Knowlton advised her. He

178

too was sore from the fighting of the last couple of days. His one source of satisfaction was that Heany was in worse shape than either Ki or himself. Although he had fully intended to kill Heany, at the last moment he had relented.

"You're right," she said. "But in the morning, I ride."

As she turned around to look at the equipment in his shop—to forestall any mention of his riding with her—Knowlton said, "Jessie, what are those papers stuffed in your pockets?"

She reached around to find out what he was talking about, and then she remembered—the letters she had taken from Goodpaster's desk. She took them out and unfolded them, a dozen pieces of paper in all, and read them with growing astonishment.

"Oh, my God, Dale. Look at this." She showed him one of the letters; it had been written by Dudley Kelso, addressed to the scheming carnival owner. In it Kelso told Goodpaster that he had wired the Circle Star ranch in Texas, and summoned Jessie Starbuck to Gilead.

"It was Kelso," Jessie breathed in amazement. "He was in touch with Goodpaster all along—that's how the son of a bitch knew about the oil in Beacon."

Incredulous, Jessie examined the other correspondence. There was a copy of a letter Goodpaster had drafted to a Mr. F. Wilhelm in Chicago, outlining the plan to take over Beacon and lure Jessie Starbuck into a trap. He specifically commended Kelso for his "loyalty and valuable services" to the cartel. Here was proof positive that the Starbuck employee had been in league with her enemies for many months—and was no doubt paid well for his services.

"And Goodpaster had him rubbed out when he was no longer useful to the plan," Knowlton said. "I swear, I had no idea, Jessie. Kelso sure fooled me."

"He fooled us all," she said. "Most of all, he fooled himself, I suppose."

"Poor bastard. He got in too deep."

179

"The cartel plays for keeps, Dale," she told him.

"With men like Goodpaster to do their dirty business for them."

"Like the men who killed my father," she said, tears gathering in her eyes.

"Damn, Jessie, if only I'd been more awake, I could have saved us a lot of trouble."

"It's not your fault, Dale. I would never have guessed Kelso had anything to do with them—especially after he was killed. He did his job too well, and they had to get rid of him." It took her a while to absorb this latest shock. The events of the past week now fell into place more neatly, and she could trace them all back to the hated cartel. It made her more anxious than ever to find Goodpaster and question him, to get closer to the source of so much grief and mayhem for her and those close to her.

For the rest of the night, Jessie was restless. She checked on Ki every hour. He was resting comfortably, and Yvonne was a vigilant nurse. She could trust her companion to the girl's care—and that eased her mind somewhat. For a few hours she slept fitfully, rising before sunup to prepare her gear.

She oiled and cleaned her .38 Colt, which her father had converted to the smaller caliber from a .44 model, to give her the power and range of the bigger gun without the recoil. Giving the same attention to her new .44-40 Winchester, she wiped the long barrel till it shone and removed every particle of dust from its workings. It was difficult to keep her mind from wandering. So much had happened in so short a time that she was still trying to sort it all out. But whatever her state of mind, Goodpaster dominated Jessie's thoughts. How could one man wreak such wide-ranging havoc? Well, whatever his motivation—whether it was power or money or simple bloodlust—she'd make him pay for it. She would make certain he was brought to justice, or else died a slow and painful death. The thought gave her

180

no pleasure, but it was something that must be done—and soon.

Knowlton, Yvonne, and Ki were all asleep as Jessie gathered up her weapons and her canteen. She found a cafe that opened early and stopped for cup of strong black coffee to help her stay awake. Then she returned to the livery and saddled up the same brown gelding that had served her so well yesterday. It was a fine animal and—she'd give Goodpaster's men credit—it had been well taken care of. She rode out of the quiet town in the same direction the carnival owner and the half-breed named Steel Knife had taken, heading toward the camp.

The morning was solemnly beautiful, the sun just cresting the eastern horizon and casting pink and gold fingers of light over the land. Once outside of town it grew even more peaceful as she covered the first mile of flat, open, green countryside. Steeled for danger as she was, Jessie could not ignore the natural grandeur of the land that spread out before her as if on some finely woven tapestry from a faraway place and time.

Cautiously she approached the campsite where she and Knowlton had been held prisoners. She listened carefully for any sound of life, but heard only the soft chirping of birds in the distant trees. Her Winchester at the ready, Jessie rode into the camp itself. It was deserted. Three fresh mounds of earth testified to the death of some of Goodpaster's men in yesterday's gun battle. There was no sign of life in or around the wagons. Perhaps some of the men were staying in town, perhaps the others had fled in directions unknown. All that was left was an eerie, ghostly assembly of uninhabited wagons.

It occurred to Jessie then that this "carnival" had been a hastily assembled show to serve as a front for Goodpaster's other activities. She passed Dr. Elihu Keith's medicine wagon and peered inside. No sign of the good doctor.

The lifelessness of the place began to affect her, sending

181

a chill up her back. Then suddenly, unmistakably, she felt the presence of someone else in the camp.

The wagons' shadows were long in the early light. The birds had stopped singing. Utterly alone, Jessie nonetheless knew that somebody else was there. She reined her mount around and walked it back toward Goodpaster's wagon.

At first she wasn't sure what it was lying there on the carnival master's steps. But as she came closer she recognized it—or him—Goodpaster's corpse. His fine clothes were tattered and bloody. Jessie dismounted. She kept the rifle crooked in her arm. The gelding remained quiet, even in the presence of death. She stepped closer, then jumped back in alarm when a figure moved out from behind the wagon.

Steel Knife stood no more than fifteen feet from her, his dark face a mask of menace. He was unarmed except for the long bowie knife in its belt sheath.

"He's dead," the half-breed said.

"I can see that," said Jessie, her heart racing and sweat slicking the palms of her hands.

"I killed him."

"I'm sure you did," she said.

"You wounded him as he rode away from the town."

Jessie remembered that she thought she had hit Goodpaster with her last shot. "Was he hurt badly?"

"No, a small wound in his shoulder. He would have lived."

"Why did you kill him?" she asked.

"He deserved to die. He would have killed me one day, if I had not killed him first."

"That's no reason."

"Reason enough. You rode after us today to kill him, didn't you?"

"If I had to, I would have killed him. I'd rather have taken him back alive. He would have been brought to trial."

"But he is dead now." The tall half-breed's flinty gray

eyes were leveled directly at hers. "Were you going to kill me too?"

"If I had to," Jessie said. "You murdered Kelso."

"Kelso also deserved to die. He betrayed you."

"I know. But he too should have been tried. That's the way the law works."

"The white man's law is a farce. Law is for lawyers and judges, not for the people. I spit on the white man's law."

"You're part white yourself."

"The part of me I hate is white. I do not live the way of the white man."

"But you take his money. You kill for him. Is that the Indian's way?"

"It is the way for many of us these days. We are professional fighting men. I work for the white man, I take his money, and I spit in his face."

"What do you do when you're not spitting or killing, Steel Knife?"

Jessie was afraid that she had angered the half-breed, as a fierce cloud passed over his face. He said, "Your words make a mockery of me. I have killed men for mocking words."

"Why do you talk to me instead of trying to kill me, then?"

"I came here because I knew you would be here. I brought this man back for you to see that I killed him. That is all. Do you want to bring me in for trial now?"

She realized that he was making a joke; though underlying the joke was a serious challenge to her sense of duty and justice. "No," Jessie said. "I don't want to bring you in. He was the man I wanted." She pointed to the blood-soaked remains of Goodpaster.

"He worked for men more evil than himself," Steel Knife said.

"Yes, and those men I have dedicated my life to fighting." From her inside vest pocket, Jessie pulled out a silk

183

handkerchief with the Circle Star brand worked in lace in one corner. She went to Goodpaster's corpse and dropped the handkerchief upon it. Then she turned away in disgust and mounted her horse.

"If I see you again, Steel Knife, I will try to kill you."

"You will never see me again," he said as he disappeared behind the wagon.

Jessie reined her mount around and started on the lonely ride back to Beacon, where Ki and the others awaited her return.

LONGARM

Explore the exciting Old West with
one of the men who made it wild!

Explore the exciting Old West with one of the men who made it wild!

____ 07066-1	LONGARM ON THE MISSION TRAIL #25	$2.25
____ 06952-3	LONGARM AND THE DRAGON HUNTERS #26	$2.25
____ 06158-1	LONGARM AND THE RURALES #27	$1.95
____ 06629-X	LONGARM ON THE HUMBOLDT #28	$2.25
____ 07067-X	LONGARM ON THE BIG MUDDY #29	$2.25
____ 06581-1	LONGARM SOUTH OF THE GILA #30	$2.25
____ 06580-3	LONGARM IN NORTHFIELD #31	$2.25
____ 06582-X	LONGARM AND THE GOLDEN LADY #32	$2.25
____ 06583-8	LONGARM AND THE LAREDO LOOP #33	$2.25
____ 06584-6	LONGARM AND THE BOOT HILLERS #34	$2.25
____ 06630-3	LONGARM AND THE BLUE NORTHER #35	$2.25
____ 06953-1	LONGARM ON THE SANTA FE #36	$2.25
____ 06954-X	LONGARM AND THE STALKING CORPSE #37	$2.25
____ 07142-0	LONGARM AND THE COMANCHEROS #38	$2.25
____ 07068-8	LONGARM AND THE DEVIL'S RAILROAD #39	$2.25
____ 07069-6	LONGARM IN SILVER CITY #40	$2.25
____ 07070-X	LONGARM ON THE BARBARY COAST #41	$2.25
____ 07127-7	LONGARM AND THE MOONSHINERS #42	$2.25
____ 07091-2	LONGARM IN YUMA #43	$2.25
____ 05600-6	LONGARM IN BOULDER CANYON #44	$2.25
____ 05601-4	LONGARM IN DEADWOOD #45	$2.25
____ 05602-2	LONGARM AND THE GREAT TRAIN ROBBERY #46	$2.25
____ 05603-0	LONGARM IN THE BADLANDS #47	$2.25
____ 05604-9	LONGARM IN THE BIG THICKET #48	$2.25
____ 06250-2	LONGARM AND THE EASTERN DUDES #49	$2.25
____ 06251-0	LONGARM IN THE BIG BEND #50	$2.25
____ 06252-9	LONGARM AND THE SNAKE DANCERS #51	$2.25
____ 06253-7	LONGARM ON THE GREAT DIVIDE #52	$2.25

Available at your local bookstore or return this form to:

JOVE/BOOK MAILING SERVICE
P.O. Box 690, Rockville Center, N.Y. 11570

Please send me the titles checked above. I enclose _____
Include 75¢ for postage and handling if one book is ordered; 50¢ per book for
two to five. If six or more are ordered, postage is free. California, Illinois, New
York and Tennessee residents please add sales tax.

NAME _____

ADDRESS _____

CITY_____ STATE/ZIP_____

Allow six weeks for delivery.

6